For Pam

Sacrifice

Enjoy!

Book One of
The Last Forever

Kelly Komm

Kelly Komm

Copyright © 2007 by Kelly Komm

ISBN 0-7414-4254-X

Published by:

PUBLISHING.COM

1094 New DeHaven Street, Suite 100
West Conshohocken, PA 19428-2713
Info@buybooksontheweb.com
www.buybooksontheweb.com
Toll-free (877) BUY BOOK
Local Phone (610) 941-9999
Fax (610) 941-9959

Printed in the United States of America

Printed on Recycled Paper

Published December 2007

Thank You...

This book would never have come to life had it not been for several people:

To the daring "prelims": Sherene Khaw, Christal Cam, Cheryl Komm, and Harris and Karen Christian. Also, a huge thanks to CKT. *Your encouragement and honesty is the glue within this book.*

To the authors who unknowingly kept me going, some with their insight and encouragement, others with their sheer talent and inspiration. Juliet Marillier, Barbara Smith, Lynn Flewelling, Lyle Weis and Cheryl Kaye Tardif. *Thank you for helping me achieve my dream.*

To my amazing family, who not only put up with the many days of endless "book" talk, but also helped me to really believe in myself. *I can never thank you enough.*

Lastly, this book is in part, dedicated to my husband Kyle. *Thank you for believing in me, loving me, and cooking for me. You rock my world.*

It is also dedicated to Arnold Rorke. Once, Uncle Arnie asked me how my book was coming along and I, trying to be impressive, told him how many words I was up to. He cleverly told me to stop counting my words, or I would never get anything done. He passed away the day I completed this novel. *We all miss you so much—your memory gives us all strength.*

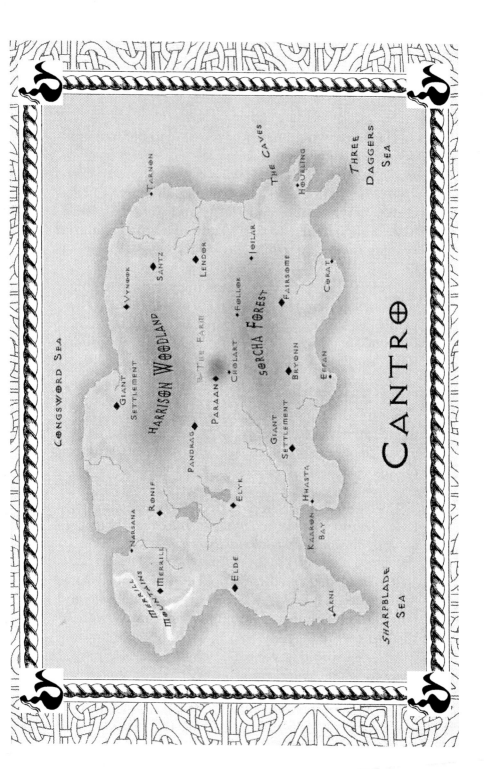

Sacrifice:
verb trans
1 to offer (something or somebody) as a sacrifice.
2 to give up or lose (something) for the sake of an ideal
or end.
-The New Penguin English Dictionary

Prologue

A red screen of blood clouded her vision, and again she heard that screaming—a horrific wailing that tugged at the soul. Although fear and fatigue weighed her down, she knew she must press on. Looking around, she saw nothing but smoke and flame. Bodies littered the once lush, green earth.

Run!

Her left leg was heavy from the injury and she feverishly realized she could be dying. Her eyes grew drowsy and everything slowed. Suddenly, all she could hear were her ragged breaths.

In. Out.

The world started to tilt and the ground furiously rushed up to greet her. The rocky surface met her face with brutal force—slicing her open and puncturing her right eye. She felt no pain. A stench of rotting mulch wafted over her as a pair of dark boots approached. She looked up and her vision blurred. Then she smiled defiantly, her white teeth crimson with blood.

The beast opened its repulsive maw to speak.

"Ssseekra," it hissed. "*Bitch.*" A metallic voice merely an echo inside her head. "Euy lentos shuy vagun."

You will die by my hand.

Her smirk grew.

"Nyut," she replied smugly. "*Come.*"

Chapter One

The blackness that followed the dream was always suffocating. Nell's heart beat at a pace so strong it felt as if it would pulse clean out of her chest. She sat upright in bed; sweat beading down her jaw line, her clean-shaven head sticky with the night's terror. Slowly peeling her eyes open, she half expected to see the dark figure. Instead, an earthen wall bathed in silvery moonlight greeted her.

Realizing she was still holding her breath, she exhaled loudly. She licked her cracked lips and looked around her bedroom for comfort. Weathered books sat randomly about the room and depleted candles left melted wax on worn wooden chests. Other than these, the room was undisturbed.

She shed her mantle and swung her feet to the side, sitting on the edge of the bed for a moment. Then she stood and walked to the window. She gazed out at the fields until her breathing finally slowed.

Their land was vast. When she reached her hand out the window, she could point to a tree and cover it with her finger. Twin moons lit the land all the way from the cottage, over the farm, right to the tip of the Harrison Woodland. Silvery dots of moonbeam pierced the fertile grounds, illuminating their usual vibrancy.

Her sleepy eyes sharpened as a movement streaked

out from the depths of the forest. Quickly, she grabbed the wooden sword she had hidden under her bed. Then she crouched beneath the window, shifting her weight from foot to foot, as her eyes darted over the windowsill, searching for more movement.

A black flash leapt unannounced toward her.

Nell gasped, jumped back and swung her sword wildly out the window.

"Mew!" the cat mocked. It jumped up onto the sill; its quick paws playfully capturing its prey.

Nell glared at her kitten and the beetle it had caught. Feeling foolish, she looked down at the pathetic stick she had carved out of firewood. She had always been drawn to swords, though her guardian never allowed her to use one.

"An Elf has no need for such things," Garick once said. He continued to have her train with the bow, even though she was quite poor with it.

Ignoring his wishes, she had searched for wood of the right length, and then carefully sneaked out her window, night after night, to cut away at it. The wooden sword was not glorious in design, but she was able to dream with it. Far away lands, daring fights. It was a wayward fantasy, but it suited her just fine.

Now, staring at the cat, she knew something important was coming—she could feel it. Unsure if it was just vigorous wishing or a premonition of sorts, she remained cynical of the thought.

She examined the tool in her hand, her scepticism rising. She vowed to go out at dawn, before Garick awoke and train some more. She slid the sword back under her bed and crawled under the covers. Sighing, she closed her eyes and snuggled into the down-filled pillow. Faerytale dreams were fun, but nothing beat a warm bed.

The morning burst open with the sun's appearance through Garick's bedroom window. Rays of sunlight pawed at his eyelids, gently rousing him. He raised his arms above his head and stretched out his body. Thrusting off the blankets, he sighed and opened his sleep-crusted eyes.

Rubbing them, he sat upright and yawned loudly. He looked around his bedroom, still dazed from a long night's restless dreaming. The dreams had started coming to him with the last moon. He had not spoken to Nell about them. There was no reason to alarm the girl. He knew there would soon be more than enough to speak about, for *it* was coming.

He shook his head to rattle himself free of such thoughts that early in the day. He walked to the washbasin in the corner of his room and undressed.

Absent-mindedly, he sung a tune while he washed.

"The Fae folk come to help you when hope is all but lost. High is the risk of action, but even higher is the cost."

Dry, Garick dressed in his work clothes, which were similar to the traditional Elvish wrap, but made of a more versatile fabric. Reaching down, he donned his slippers.

A quick glance out the window revealed a figure sprinting across the grounds, heading toward the well. He stumbled in his panic as he ran to the window. Relief swept over him when he saw that it was Nell.

"Garick, you silly arse! You thought someone was here for her after all this time." Sighing, he ran a hand over his hairless scalp and strode out the door.

Nell stood in the field over the hill from the cottage. The warm wind ran around her like a playful child. Her arms outstretched, she inclined her head to the Goddess above. The beige wrap she wore flapped softly against her pale skin.

No other Elf had such colourless skin. In contrast, her guardian's skin was dark as the night sky.

Her mint-green eyes were squeezed shut to the radiant sun when she sensed Garick's approach.

Today. Something is going to happen today.
Tilting her head forward, she drew her arms closed, smiled at her guardian and opened her eyes. Her gaze followed down his arms, noting that he was dragging two gleaming swords.
Her smile swiftly diminished.
Where did he get those? What is going on?
Garick hated swords, which was why she had hid her substitute from him all this time. In fact, he had always been reluctant to even let her near them when they saw the odd one at a shop in the village. It was a widely known fact that Elves were clumsy with a sword, as Garick demonstrated by the unceremonious way he hauled them.
"Take this," Garick commanded.
Stepping toward her, he thrust the hilt of a sword into her hands. It dazzled cobalt in the morning sun and the blade shone magnificently.
"I do not understand," she said.
Her guardian nodded toward the weapon, a look of sad acceptance on his face. "You will."
She lifted the glorious instrument—its weight feeling strangely appropriate in her hands. Feeling empowered, she brought the weapon higher, its lightness surprising her. She began to swing it, whipping the lethal blade back and forth. Lunging and feinting, she danced with the power the sword released. An unearthly sense of belonging enveloped her, bringing out natural instincts she had never known she had harboured.
As she unintentionally performed with the sword, Nell grinned, and Garick, mesmerized by the display before him, noticed he had been holding his breath.
He exhaled.
Nell stopped at the sound. Her face was flushed and her eyes sparkled in a way he had only seen once before, many cycles earlier. He stared at her, realizing this long-dreaded day had arrived.
She is still so young.
Her figure was strong from their farm work, yet still

clung to its child-like frame. Her face held an innocence he knew would soon disappear. She was on the brink of womanhood.

Looking over her delicate build, he felt a twinge of loss.

Everything will change.

He took a deep breath. "I have a story for you, Nelhua."

Nell stopped swinging immediately.

After they stuck the swords in the ground—the hilts standing upright and proud—he placed his arm on her back and led her over the hill to their home.

As they walked to the cottage, Nell was nervous. Garick very rarely used her full name. In fact, she could not remember the last time he had. The scent of fresh lavender wafted over them as they walked through the kitchen, arriving in the small dining hall.

Garick pointed to a chair. "Sit, Nell. I will fetch us something to drink." He disappeared into the kitchen.

From the centrepiece, she grabbed some walnuts to nibble on while waiting for his return.

Why is he being so formal?

Garick was always the first to joke and play. He had been her guardian and only real friend since her parents had drowned when she was three.

She supposed hers was a fun—if sheltered—life, where they went into Paraan, the nearby village, only occasionally. Everything she knew she had learned from Garick and from the books that adorned their many shelves. Their cottage was comfortable and tiny, housing two bedrooms, a dining hall and a kitchen. It was cozy and exactly all they needed.

Garick returned with two glasses of Tartwine, a remarkable drink she had experienced only a few times in her life.

She watched as he placed a glass in front of her.

"Have a sip, Nell," he recommended, throwing back a hearty gulp.

His face showed stress and something she had never

seen on her easy-going guardian's features—dread.

Something is very wrong.

A surge of panic froze in her chest and she gingerly took a sip, letting the wine warm her insides.

"Nell," Garick began as he sat across from her. "I am going to tell you a story. It is not a fable or myth, but truth. It is about our land, Cantro, and its inhabitants." He paused, looking distressed. "In the name of Saros," he muttered, sipping his wine. "Where to start?"

She waited and watched intently.

Garick placed his clenched hands on the thick wooden table and cleared his throat. "You understand how the Goddess Saros created all living things—good and bad? How she created Elf, Dragon, Dwarf, Merfolk, Sarkian, Giant, Garshu and all the animals and plants that adorn our world?"

She nodded. She remembered learning all of this, not to mention seeing several of those races in Paraan, on their rare trips.

"Saros also created another race, one that many believe has been wiped out. The Garshu were enemies of this race, and there were many wars and horrific battles between the two. In the end, it was thought this other race was destroyed. It is rumoured there are small bands of them roving around, looking for others like them. And the Garshu are still hunting them."

"What race was this?" she asked, thoroughly engrossed in his tale.

"They are called Humans."

She squinted, certain she had heard that name before.

"Garick, when I was small," she said, thinking back, "I was playing in your room and I picked the lock to your closet, remember?"

A corner of Garick's mouth lifted. "I remember."

She looked at him. "I found a few pages with names and sketches on them. I am sure I remember that name being on one sheet."

He nodded. "Yes, that is right. After that incident, I always told you that I keep that closet booby-trapped—

just to keep you out."

Nell playfully threw a walnut at him. "I have been terrified of that room ever since, you deceiver." She giggled.

A loud *crack* interrupted their fun. They looked out the window and saw a downpour erupt from the now blackened skies. Lightening flashed in the distance and thunder splintered once more.

Garick rose from his chair and closed the shutters.

"Nell…there is something you need to know. I was not sure when to tell you…until today."

He inhaled deeply and gave her a sad look. He feared the words he was about to say.

"Nelhua, you are Human—not Elvish, as I have always told and raised you to be. You are not of the Shanasar Clan, as I am. Your real name is Nelhua Lily Sahnatru. I am so sorry I could not tell you earlier, but it would have been dangerous. It is better this way. Believe me."

Thinking she should be confused and beyond angry, Nell—oddly enough—felt neither. There were so many emotions pulsing through her that she could not focus on even one.

They sat in silence.

"Nell, please say something," Garick asked after a few minutes had passed.

She remained silent.

He noticed his glass was now dry. Hers was still full.

"Look, I am going to get some more wine. I will be right back." With glass in hand, he shuffled toward the kitchen.

He felt awful. He had always wanted to tell Nell the truth. He had planned the discussion in his mind a hundred times, but he could never chance endangering her. Although he had been commanded to tell her, he could not bring himself to do it. It never seemed to be the right time.

Until now.

He poured more wine and forced the cork back in the large jug. Lost in thought, he picked up his glass and headed back to the dining room. Once seated, he sipped his drink, until he noticed something that made his heart skip a beat.

Nell's seat was empty.

"Nell!" he yelled, bursting from his chair. "Nell, where did you go?"

He sprinted from the shadowed hall to her room, calling her name repeatedly. Finally, he saw light coming from his own room, the last open doorway in the hall. He stepped inside, knowing instinctively what he would find.

Light radiated from the far end of his bedroom, from under the crack of the small door to his closet. He flung open the door and found Nell huddled on the floor, a coloured sketch in her hand and a lit candle beside her.

She looked at him, tears streaking down her face. She thrust the picture at him, sobbing. "Why does this Human look like me? I remember finding it when I was small, and I never asked you about it. You told me there were no pictures of my parents, but there is. This is my mother, is it not?"

"Nell, I…uh…" He crouched and hugged her, but she tensed at his touch. "I am so sorry I could not tell you. It was too dangerous."

He sat down across from her, glancing nervously at the back wall of the closet. A thick wine-coloured drape hung ominously behind them.

He looked at Nell. "That is a picture of your mother. I could not show you because you would have seen she was Human."

His gaze flickered, resting on the face of the woman in the picture. "I have kept you looking as Elvish as possible for so long, by shaving your hair and giving you certain clothes." He snorted. "Elves do not even *have* hair. Have you ever seen me shave my head the way we do yours? I could not tell you the truth. You would not have understood why your hair grew. When it comes in, I am sure it will look like this." He gestured to the picture.

Nell stared at the sketch. The artist had used a beautiful hue of ink, and her mother's crimson hair was astonishing. She had never seen red hair before. She smiled faintly through her tears, noticing she had her mother's light green eyes and plump pink lips.

"I can grow my hair out now?" she asked, subdued.

"Oh my, yes!" Garick laughed with relief.

They sat for a long moment and he was relieved once he sensed the unfamiliar tensions finally leave. He opened his mouth to speak.

Nell beat him to it.

"Garick, why was it dangerous to tell me the truth?"

He looked at her, inhaling deeply, then briefly eyed the drape hanging beside them. "Let us get out of here first and I will tell you more."

After they emerged from the closet, he securely locked the door. He took the key out of the handle and hung it back on its hook, halting momentarily to glance at Nell. Changing his mind, he stuffed the key into his pocket.

When they sat down on his bed, Garick took her hands and gazed into her eyes. Nell saw a sadness she had never noticed before.

"Your parents did not drown," he told her in a gentle voice. "The Garshu murdered them."

He closed his eyes, remembering the day his life changed, twelve cycles earlier...

Chapter Two

The water was calm in Kaaron Bay, not far from the village of Hhasta. Coada and his wife Illedria walked hand-in-hand to the water's edge, where a fingertip of soft white sand kissed the ocean. They knelt down to open up their hand-woven net. Illedria's ability to weave fishing nets was beyond compare in their small village.

Unequalled as well was her beauty. There was something special in Illedria's bloodline that accounted for her rare and astounding loveliness. Petite in height, with a solid yet graceful frame, Illedria's figure was exquisite. Her flowing crimson mane caught the eyes of any who gazed upon her.

However, the few who seized a glance from her were truly fortunate. For those eyes—Illedria's eyes—could stop a man's heart cold in his chest. A gripping sea-foam green, they held more passion and meaning than anyone had ever seen. It changed a person, looking into those eyes.

"Coada, are you ready?" Illedria asked.

"Ready as ever, my love."

They tossed the net far out into the water and drove it under. Pulling it back, they could already feel the weight of dinner in their hands.

"Mama!" a voice squealed in delight.

Illedria set down the catch and turned. Her young

daughter ran toward her, red curls bouncing in the sunlight.

"Nelhua!" Illedria exclaimed, her arms outstretched for the little girl. She lifted the child and spun her around in the air.

Coada tied up the net, smiling at the sight of his wife and daughter.

"Hi, moonbeam," he cooed, tousling Nell's bright hair.

An older, gruff-looking Dwarven woman, followed by a handsome young Elf, sauntered toward them.

"Lowla," Illedria called. "How was your visit to the village?"

"Ah, mum, as always—a pleasure." Lowla's hardened expression melted somewhat and she leaned in so only Illedria could hear. "The fine-looking innkeeper tha' fancies me was waitin' for us an' he cut me some posies." Straightening, she resumed her brusque expression. "The carpenter couldna' come straight away about the cart, so he sent 'is son." She turned. "Wha' was yer name again, boy?"

"Garick, mum," the Elf answered, sheepishly glancing at Coada.

The family headed toward their home, catch in tow. Lowla walked in front, her large strides leading the way, while Garick trailed behind.

"I'll start dinner, mum," Lowla announced, grabbing the heap of fish from Illedria's hands. "You shouldna' be lifting such things in yer condition." She gestured to Illedria's swollen belly.

"Lowla, I worked all nine moons carrying Nell in my womb." Illedria caressed the pale blue fabric that clung to her stomach. "This one's no different."

Lowla grunted disapprovingly and walked away.

"It is an honour to meet you, sir," Garick told Coada while he shook his hand vigorously. "Your exceptional skill with a sword is well known."

"Well, tell me more," Coada teased, throwing an arm around the young Elf's shoulders as they went off to inspect the broken cart.

Illedria picked up Nell and began to brush the dirt from the child's hands. "I told you not to play with—"

She broke off mid-sentence as a feeling of dread engulfed her. She noticed Coada staring at her, the feeling taking him as well. Even Nell sensed it, and clung tightly to her mother.

An enormous, deafening boom suddenly blew Illedria and Nell into the air and slammed them to the ground. Fire and smoke began to billow up fiercely through the cottage roof, as though it were eager to breathe unsoiled air.

With some effort, Illedria raised her head.

Coada and the Elf were running toward her.

"Illedria! Nell!" There was dire panic in Coada's voice. "What's happened?"

"I don't know," Illedria cried, standing. "Wait here with Nell. I need to see if Lowla is all right."

She placed a protective hand on her belly and started toward the burning cottage.

Hordes of vicious beasts poured down the hillside. They came like a swarm—a buzzing wave of repulsion.

"Garshu!" Illedria screamed.

The Garshu's metal boots stormed the field; they filled the smoky air with the sound of thunder.

She drew her sword instantly, as did her husband.

"Illedria, you and Nell must go," Coada told her. "You must hide."

"I will not leave you. You should know this by now."

The fierce look in her eyes told him there was no sense in arguing.

He turned to the young Elf. "Garick, take Nell and run. Go now!"

With the young girl curled up in his arms, Garick ran sprightly toward the bay and to the forest that bordered it. Behind him, he heard swords clashing and the battle hisses of the Garshu.

Nell began to cry. "Mama! Papa!" Her arms stretched out toward the sound of the battle.

Garick spotted a sheltering thistonberry bush and

crawled underneath it. Luckily, its large indigo leaves provided ample coverage for them. He prayed they would be overlooked, since they were on the border of the forest.

There must be more than fifty Garshu.

He knew that Humans had an unparalleled talent with swords, but two against more than fifty were horrible odds.

Since the wars between Garshu and Humans had begun, few Humans had survived, due to the new pyro-weapons the Garshu were constantly inventing. The Controlice that had once acted as the dominating force in Cantro was no more. The Garshu overthrew their governing ways early on, so they could freely attack settlements.

They were multiplying much faster too.

Garshu had two females—no more, no less—that laid hundreds of black eggs every moon. They could choose the sex of their eggs, and they created them at an astonishing rate. If a female, a Garshula, were to die, the other Garshula would sense it and produce a female to replace her. A shiny, *white* egg.

Leaves crunched under heavy boots.

The child quieted, as if sensing the need for secrecy.

"They mussst be in here." A Garshulan's hissing voice echoed at the edge of the forest. "There wasss an Elfff and the Human offfsssspring. Fffind them. Kill them."

Garick held his breath. Nell's powerful eyes looked up at him, wide and so like her mothers. He knew that even at her tender age, she understood him.

"Shh," he whispered.

The Garshulan's perverted breathing neared the spot where they were hiding. Garick could hear him sniffing the air for their scent. His heart ached in his chest, swelling with colossal fear. They would have absolutely no chance. They would die. It was certain.

He strained to hear, but could not make out any swords battling in the distance, so there was no hope of rescue.

Are Coada and Illedria already dead?

He watched through the branches as the creature moved only three strides away.

The Garshulan's pointed ears stuck out past the coarse, black fuzz that adorned his head. His beady eyes focused on the forest around him and veins stood out all over his powerfully built grey torso. A necklace of bones and small fingers hung from his thick neck. Drool trickled off the fangs that hung out over his nauseating lips and Garick knew he was staring at a walking nightmare.

Abruptly, the Garshulan stopped, his ears pricking up at another sound. Without warning, his head whipped around and stared fiercely at the thistonberry bush.

He could see them. Garick was sure of it.

The creature's translucent eyes narrowed. Then he proceeded toward them.

"Arrhh!" Coada bellowed as he streaked, blood-soaked and battle-worn, through the trees and toward the Garshulan. His sword came down on the beast, cleanly removing its head.

Suddenly, Garshu hissing could be heard in the forest.

"Garick!" Coada's voice dripped with alarm. "Nell!"

"Sir?" Garick said, rising from behind the bush.

"You must go!"

A squealing object flew toward them. It detonated in midair, blinding Garick briefly. Instant fire was generated, levelling most of the trees nearby, and Garick and Nell were propelled back into the bush.

Then the Garshu appeared. They walked through the flames, the fire having no effect on them.

"At lassst he isss dead," one announced, staring triumphantly at Coada's motionless body.

"What offf the Elffff?" another asked. "Hisss remainsss are not here. He musssst have run."

Shivering in terror, Garick held Nell close.

"Ah, he isss no concern of oursss. Let him go."

"And the Human child?"

"With no fffood, ssshelter or guardian, it will die painfffully in thisss fffforesssst. Thand will be pleasssed to hear we have ffffinally killed thisss Human. Do not mention the Elffff—or the child."

The Garshu stalked away through the dying flames.

Garick and Nell lingered until all sounds of Garshu had long since faded. They slowly emerged from the bush, their bodies covered in dirt and sweat. As soon as the fire dwindled, he placed Nell by a tree, letting the child curl up in the old roots. "Stay here, little one."

He slowly made his way to Coada's charred body. It lay amid the smouldering wood, and Garick found it difficult to believe that not an hour earlier, this blackened mass was a strong and mighty legend. Coada's once shoulder-length hair was now singed and melted to his skull. His noble jaw now hung limp, gaping open. His limbs were barely attached, and tears rushed to Garick's eyes at the sight of this monstrosity.

Yet, a scrap of life remained in the stoic Human.

"Garick," Coada croaked. "Please...don't let them harm Nelhua. Tell her! You know who she is. Do not let them harm her because of it. Make sure she never forgets that we loved her more...than...any—" His last breath escaped and death forever glazed over his dark eyes.

Garick's heart broke at the sight and he thought he might vomit. He looked over at Nell. She was watching from a distance, her bottom lip quivering.

She knows.

By the time they reached the remains of the cottage, the Garshu were gone, except for the dead that littered the blood-soaked ground. The Human couple certainly had not gone quietly or without a fight.

Garick set Nell down and inspected the field. The cottage was only smoking timbers and ash. He could see Lowla's remains strewn in the doorway. Illedria's body was gone.

He noticed a twitching Garshulan, but it was the creature's sword that made his breath stop. A piece of light blue cloth clung faithfully to the blade. He recognized it immediately. This fabric had been torn from Illedria's lovely body.

A glimmer in the grass caught his eye.

Illedria's sword lay abandoned not far from the dying Garshulan, and he plucked it from the ground.

He fixed his eyes on Nell and pity for the little girl swelled inside him. She was playing with some ash on the ground, a quiet tune on her lips. Her tone was dull, comatose, as though her very soul had been raped. She had nothing left. She was alone.

"Well, now she has *me*," he said.

Holding the sword in one hand, he scooped her up in the other. Nell rested her head on his shoulder, her eyes never leaving her mother's sword.

Chapter Three

Garick's eyelids fluttered open as he finished delivering the distressing tale to a now grown Nelhua. Weary lines pulled at the corners of his tear-filled eyes.

Nell's face revealed a pain that even she could not comprehend. She was too stunned even to cry. She stood, shaking, then left his room.

He let her go. He understood she needed time. He had suddenly altered her entire existence.

Nell walked doggedly through the cottage and burst through the side door, frustrated. She headed toward the well. It was about thirty paces from the door and gave a glorious view of their land from atop a hill.

She felt numb. Each step was a conscious process of placing one foot down after the other, so that walking became a mechanical chore rather than the effortless movement of the past.

When she reached the well, she leaned against the aging stone, grasped the edge and stared down into the murky darkness of the hole. Her vision blurred with emotional tears.

"Everything is different now."

Her parents had been brutally hunted and murdered. She was Human—a race she had barely known existed an hour ago.

"Who am I?" she wept. "*What* am I?"

Such questions had never crossed her innocent mind.

Garick had given up his life to raise her. He had only known her for moments before the responsibility to care for her was thrust upon him. She now understood his reluctance to tell her about her past.

Now that she had been told about the day her parents were murdered, she could vaguely remember certain things. She remembered the sound of the Garshu. It made her skin crawl, as though a hundred insects were exploring her. She recalled a vague vision of Lowla's thick Dwarven hands. She could almost remember their warmth; her father's smile—oh, what a smile! Her mother's hair—the soft radiance of it.

Aware of her tears, she wiped them away and emptied her mind. She returned to the field that she and Garick had visited just that morning and plucked one of the swords from the earth. Its blade glistened in the sun.

She closed her eyes, thinking of the sketching. "I miss you, mother."

She knew her mother could hear her…somehow.

Garick appeared in the cabin doorway. He strolled toward her, somewhat hesitant, and then pulled the other sword from the ground. "Want to have a go at it?"

"Absolutely," she replied, confidence apparent in her drying eyes.

They took their opening stances.

"Go!" Garick yelled.

They started toward each other, taking slow steps. Nell brought the sharp blade down near his arm, causing him to counteract with a forceful upward swing. He was afraid of knocking her right off her feet, but she proved to shock him once more. As the blades were about to meet, she thwarted him with a solid block, halting him abruptly. The sun surveyed their movements, lighting their swords with silvery magnificence. They broke apart and took a step away from each other.

"You are doing well," he said with a grunt.

To Nell, his look read pure condescendence.

She smirked at him. "Aye."

She felt renewed at the sport—and in general. Her spirit exploded with ancient knowledge, and it trickled through to her fingertips.

"Again," she said.

Garick yelled as he aimed the tip of his sword at her. He darted forward, but she ran her blade around his, easily disarming the attempt. She swung at his right side. He blocked it. She immediately tried the same on his left. He stumbled. Her speed and accuracy had taken him aback. She saw his unsteady footing and whipped her blade around to the right side of his neck. She halted the edge a finger's width from his skin.

"I would say I am doing very well," she said, looking at her guardian proudly.

They sank to the ground, panting with exhaustion.

Nell noticed Garick's laboured attempts at catching his breath. Surprisingly, she breathed quite normally.

She glanced at her sword. "I do not know what came over me, Garick."

"Well, perhaps your intuition kicked in when I told you that you were Human. You are now doing what naturally comes to you."

"Intuition? I am not familiar with this word."

Garick scratched his bald head. "Hmm…I suppose it is like unconsciously knowing something. Like when you have a feeling something is going to happen. Or when you do something instinctively, like swordplay. Humans are the only race that has intuition." He smiled. "But *all* races have their secret talents."

Nell leaned closer, thirsty for more information. "Why do the Garshu hate Humans so? What did they—I mean, *we*—do to them?"

Garick did his best to answer her endless questions. He told her that power, or the desire for it, had turned the once-docile Garshu slaves into a murderous horde.

"Do Merfolk, Sarkians and Dragons still exist? I have never seen them."

"Nor will you," he scoffed. "Merfolk are still rumoured to be causing trouble in the waters, though sightings are rare. Dragons have not been seen since the wars between Humans and Garshu began, but it is assumed that they are still living somewhere in their caves. Sarkians, however, are quite common to see. There are even some in Paraan."

Nell grinned. "Really?"

They spoke for many hours, discussing and theorizing on numerous topics regarding Humans, Elves and other creatures of Cantro. By the time their conversation had lapsed, it was dark outside and the twin moons were rising above the trees in the Harrison Woodland.

Garick sighed. "I think there has been enough said today. We will talk more tomorrow."

After a light dinner and an attempt at the chores that were abandoned that day, Nell lay in bed, thinking. There was so much she did not know about Humans. She resolved to ask Garick first thing in the morning to take her into town to the local bookshoppe. She wanted to read everything they had about her race.

She fell asleep that evening with visions of her parents in her mind. She smiled all night long.

Garick awoke to the sunrise barely lighting his room and the scent of herbs teasing his senses. After he changed his clothes, he headed into the kitchen where Nell was busy preparing breakfast. She had already gathered eggs, squeezed fresh juice and chopped newly plucked herbs. A bowl of rising dough sat on the table, with gathered fruit beside it.

He stifled a yawn. "You are up early. Did you sleep all right?"

Nell faced him, her eyes bright and her skin flushed with excitement. "I had the best sleep of my life. I awoke feeling so refreshed and alert."

"Aye, and you just thought you would make breakfast at dawn?"

"Well, since I was awake, I thought it would be nice to make breakfast for you." She peeked at him and smirked sweetly. "All right, I was hoping you would do me a wee favour. It is nothing really."

He eyed her, suspicious. "So what is this *wee* favour?"

"Well...I was hoping you would take me into the village today. I wanted to visit the bookshoppe." She raised her chin. "I would like to read more about the Human race—*my* race."

Garick grinned. "I am glad you are embracing this so vigorously. Not many could deal with such matters so well. You are a special person." His expression grew serious. "However, I am not certain we should be heading into town so soon. There are a few things I would like us to focus on before you make your debut."

Their eyes met.

Nell was clearly disappointed.

"Let us eat," he said with a sigh. "We shall do our chores, then go play with some swords."

Once they finished eating breakfast, Nell rushed outside to complete her chores. She took care of the animals, few as they had. Their horses were easy enough to maintain, but their Buktrana was her favourite.

Buktranas vaguely resembled seals, except they had overflowing coats of lavender fur and three legs, which were thick as tree trunks. The creatures were mostly used for labour, such as pulling carts, although it was discovered early on that the animals had other uses. Their urine was the best fertilizer ever seen. In turn, crops grew sturdy and fast. Some of their urine-rich soil was sold regularly, gaining high profits each time. The problem, however, was that going near the creatures was practically impossible, for they spooked easily and would bolt.

Once Nell became old enough, feeding and cleaning the Buktrana fell onto her shoulders, since Garick could barely get near them. She had an air about her and their Buktrana actually came to her, as though it saw her as a friend. In turn, it had become cuddly and loyal. Now that she knew she was of a different race, Nell thought it obvious why the Buktrana was calm with her and not with Garick. It made her wonder if there were other creatures out there that acted differently toward Humans.

She wondered about so much now.

After her chores were finished, she went to find Garick.

"How about you practice some of the moves I showed you with your sword?" he suggested. "I am nearly through."

Her face brightening, she sprinted to the grassy hillside. Picking up her blade, she began the exercises he had shown her. She practiced a long time before she stopped to catch her breath.

Garick watched in awe, noting that Nell had inherited her mother's elegant movements, and her father's strong and swift technique.

It is as if they have reached out from the grave.

From that day on, Nell began to learn new things. She acquired knowledge from books, knowledge from Garick, and even on her own. Many of the books her guardian brought her told of a golden age when Humans co-existed with all other creatures. None, however, told her why Humans had become obsolete. Every time she asked him about it, he would just mumble something about finding her the right book, or he would change the subject.

She began to believe he did not know.

Of the many books she found, she especially took to the one on languages. As time progressed, she became fluent in various foreign tongues. She rubbed her head, enjoying the feel of soft hairs growing back as she practiced the new words.

Garick began to place little things around the house. He told her he had hidden them in the past because they were Human-related.

"It was difficult to show you certain things when they

always made reference to the very thing I was hiding from you," he said one day from the kitchen.

"What is this one?" she asked, picking up a wooden figurine that had mysteriously found its way onto the mantle.

Garick appeared in the doorway, a bowl in one hand. "That is for you. It belonged to your father. I found it in the cart with his whittling tools. I believe he was carving it for you. Or your unborn sibling." At that, he returned to the kitchen.

Nell looked at the wooden doll with renewed joy. The figurine was that of a little boy holding a fish. The face was rough and bare, for her father had not had time to create it. It was sad to think that she might have had a little brother or sister that would have played with this.

She carefully placed it back on the shelf.

"Where have you been keeping all of these trinkets and books?" she asked Garick when he reappeared.

"Oh, I have my places," he said mysteriously.

Her eyes spanned their small home. "I do not see how."

Chapter Four

Lachlin Alican Ferenwe and her twin brother raced through thick grass that textured the banks of the river that emptied into the ocean bordering their village. Liam was ahead, gesturing for her to hurry. As she ran with all her might, she looked over her shoulder and saw children from the village running too. There were dozens of them, all rushing in the same direction—to the ocean.

It was time for the migration. The cooler winds were starting to blow and all the fish would be leaving soon.

Lachlin knew exactly what the children would do. As in past years, they would scan the surface of the water for any signs of movement. Occasionally, a child would squeal, swearing that they saw a tail or a head. This was normal, and it happened every cycle. Everyone in the area knew the legends of Merfolk, and how they supposedly lived just off the coast of their village, Narsana.

Lachlin finally reached the beach and joined her brother.

Hours passed and the sky darkened.

Disappointed children disappeared one by one, leaving Lachlin and Liam perched on a rock slab that jutted out over the ocean.

"I want to see Merfolk," she whined.

Her eyes were red from fighting the urge to blink and

she was cold, for her shift was letting her feel the wind a little too much.

"It's getting dark," Liam said. "We will see nothing this cycle. We'll come next season. Nice and early."

It broke his heart telling her this, but he knew that Merfolk did not really exist. Besides, he was hungry.

His sister's eyes welled with tears as she began her descent down the huge rock. He stepped backwards, allowing her room to pass. His foot skidded on a patch of slippery moss and he landed on his rear end.

"Liam!" Lachlin cried.

When she reached his side, she helped him up, concerned. Then she saw his face. He was roaring with laughter.

"Liam!"

"Y-you thought I was g-gonna fall in!" He doubled up, clutching his stomach in delight.

Angry, she shoved him, unaware that he was standing on the moss patch. She watched in horror as her brother slid down the rock, toward the churning water. He twisted, trying to grasp anything he could, and she saw terror in his eyes.

The world slowed and Liam disappeared.

Splash!

Lachlin crawled to the edge of the rock slab. Lying flat on her stomach, she inched as far out as she could—but she saw nothing.

"Liam?"

Why hasn't he surfaced?

In the dark, she tried to make out the rocks below.

He must have been sucked between the rocks.

Sickened, she eased away from the rock and made her way down to the shore. She moved beneath the slab, peering into the shadows of the murky water.

"Liam!"

Nothing.

Panic gripped her and salty tears filled her eyes. She stubbornly wiped them away, and then ran back to the rock, hoping it would yield a miracle. On her knees, she felt her way to where Liam had gone over.

She peered over the edge.

Only the inky brine mirrored her, it was so dark outside.

Lying on the rock, she let her sorrow overtake her. Her face was cold on the stone as her tears flowed freely.

"Lachlin! Liam!"

Lachlin raised her head, just a bit.

Her parents passed by the rock, but she remained still.

I'm not returning without my brother—my twin soul.

She watched her parents' head back to the village.

Hours passed, and Lachlin thought she must be meeting death, for a bright blue light swept over her. It emanated from the water.

She pulled herself to the edge of the slab.

Below, huge snow-white eyes stared back at her.

A Mermaid!

Lachlin gawked at the creature, with its long burnt-looking hair and skin that reminded her of the icicles that hung from the trees in the wintertime. Its arms appeared to be taken from some enormous spider and sewn half-heartedly onto a wormlike frame, which past the waist yielded an iridescent thorny fin.

The Mermaid's eyes blazed with anger. "Why are you doing this?" Her voice was deep and scratchy, almost like wind squealing through a tiny window.

"Doing what?" Lachlin asked, confused.

"Why are you spoiling our water? You are plaguing it with *this*!"

The Mermaid splashed her in the face.

"Those are my tears," Lachlin said. "My brother has fallen in and...and I think he's dead. Oh! I miss him terribly!"

The Mermaid cocked her head and a terrible smile crept across her lips. "Your brother is with us now."

"Please! Give him back to me! I'll do anything."

The Mermaid's smile grew. "There is nothing you could do that is of any interest to us." She began to descend.

Lachlin sat up. "No! Please don't go. I can't live without Liam. He's the only true guide I have in life. I can't go on without him."

The creature ignored her pleas, continuing her descent.

"Wait!" Lachlin shouted. "What about some sort of bargain?"

She regretted saying the words the moment they met the air, the moment she saw the intrigue that weighed heavily in the Mermaid's eyes.

"Bargain?"

"Yes. If you give me my brother back, you may hold a life bind with me."

The Mermaid raised a silky eyebrow. "Go on."

"At any time in the future, you may call upon me for any need." Lachlin swallowed. "If my life...or death... serves your kind, I give it freely. Should I fail to honour this bind, may Saros strike me dead!" She raised an arm to the sky, and distant rumbling above was heard in agreement.

The creature's eyes gleamed, overjoyed.

"It will be your death, for we will filch your life. A life bind is an ancient agreement, but as strong now as it ever was. Be assured of the fact that you have been acquired."

The Mermaid disappeared below the surface.

The blue light grew unbearably bright, and Lachlin sat back, squeezing her eyes shut. She held up her arms, trying to block the burning radiance. A searing pain stung her neck, but she quickly set the pain aside when she felt a warm weight on her legs.

She looked down and let out a gasp. "Liam?"

A perfectly dry Liam rested his head in her lap.

"Lach?"

Lachlin's head jerked off the pillow, the memory of that terrifying day on Narsana's beach more than ten years earlier, drifting away from her.

Liam was staring at her from his bed. They slept in a

small shed that had been abandoned during the wars.

Sitting up in the straw bed, she wiped tears from her face. "Liam, I—"

"You were crying in your sleep again," he interrupted, watching her carefully.

"I was remembering that day at the beach when you fell in."

"With the Mermaid?" he teased.

"Liam, she *was* there and she saved your life. You can't even prove me wrong. You don't remember how you got out of the water."

They exchanged challenging glares.

"Besides," Lachlin continued, "you were underwater for hours. How do you explain your survival?"

She fingered the swollen stripe around her throat. It always swelled when she had the dream.

"And where did this lovely mark come from?" She looked at him expectantly.

"I…" Liam's voice trailed away.

"Yeah, you can't. So shush up."

They exchanged sly grins and slipped from their beds.

At a tender age, Lachlin and Liam had found shelter with an elderly couple after they were orphaned and forced to leave their village because of Garshu raiders. Karistaal and Peter were old, but very smart. Everyone called Karistaal *Kris*, but she secretly preferred her full name. Peter was stubbornly feisty, as some old men become when they will not accept their age. The pair believed they took care of everyone, when really they were coming into an age where they were the ones being taken care of.

With them was Treyton, a man about the twins' age, a ripe seventeen. When Liam and Lachlin escaped their village, Treyton somehow just appeared at their sides. He was strong, but jaded. Horrible things had happened to him. That much was obvious, though he never spoke of it and no one asked him to. They never talked about where they all came from. For most, it was too painful.

Bean, a boy shrouded in much mystery, completed their group. They found him when he was only five, almost eight cycles earlier. Garshu had captured him and locked him in a shed. They doused the structure with a chemical and lit it.

They left him to burn.

Peter rescued the boy, however the experience left the child horribly scarred, both mentally, but most prominently, physically. The whole of his face looked to be raw hamburger, as did the rest of his body. He grew up quiet and self-conscious. He was known to have strange bouts of bewildering madness. He would leave the group, sometimes for days, sometimes for weeks on end. He always came back, though, and acted as if everything were perfectly normal.

It was...for a while.

The twins and their companions traveled wherever their feet took them. They were a band of Humans— maybe the last ones—and they survived by their wits and blades. They grew together, enjoying each others company and surviving in their hostile world. They let their differences bring them together, while the world became harder and harder for them to endure. Nothing was easy when you were the last of your kind and constantly hunted by creatures that knew nothing of mercy or compassion.

They slept with one eye open.

And woke each day knowing it could be their last.

Chapter Five

"Ah, good morning, my dears," Karistaal greeted the twins cheerfully.

She stood outside their shack, airing out some clothes.

Lachlin tugged a pair of aged, woollen gloves onto her hands and smiled faintly, the dream still lingering in her senses.

Karistaal winked at Liam as he passed by, but her expression sharpened and she gently seized Lachlin's arm. "I heard you dreaming again. Are you all right?"

Lachlin nodded, loosening the old woman's grip. "I'm fine." She straightened and walked away.

"Did she have another one?" Peter asked, his seasoned face still dripping from his morning wash.

"No," Karistaal replied. "She had a night terror. Thank Saros it was not one of *those*."

At the well with his sister, Liam rubbed icy water into his skin, as though trying to scrub away a part of himself. He finished—his skin raw—and turned to face the vast field that lay before their camp.

On a distant hill, Bean was practicing with his sword. He was very quick for someone his age. He lunged forward with excellent technique and drew himself back with refined poise. He laced the air with the blade and it passed his perimeter with true formality. One would swear the blade was riding his skin; he brought it so close. The boy always came back from his practice, unmarked and seeping with nameless thrill.

"Aye, he's good."

Lachlin's soft voice broke Liam's trance.

"I think once he gets older, he could become the best," he said, sliding his tunic over his head. "Better than anyone left, anyhow."

Lachlin eyed Bean, a curious smirk playing at the corner of her lips. "I wonder where he gets it."

Bean left the hill and shyly approached Treyton. He blushed when he saw the twins watching him.

"Are we still leaving today?" he asked Treyton, his face glistening from the morning's efforts with the sword.

"Aye."

Treyton was packing his horse for the journey and his face showed stern apprehension. He always looked that way before they set off for new lands. It was only to be expected that they would run into the Garshu eventually.

Bean set off to pack his own horse.

Liam made his way toward Treyton. "Trey, we're going to start packing up." He leaned against the horse's flank and caressed its shiny coat.

"I'm all ready," Treyton snapped.

Liam stiffened. "Just remember what we discussed. No more of your nonsense."

"It's not nonsense!" Treyton scowled. "It's a good idea. You aren't being reasonable."

Ever since their argument several days earlier, tension was thick around the two of them.

Liam released a sigh. "Trey, I want us kept safe. I will not condone any foolish ideas that will put us in danger." He reached for his friend's shoulder. "Come, let us forget this anger, brother."

Together, they walked toward the shacks and began packing their paltry belongings.

Nell woke peacefully, her eyes adjusting to the sunlight that illuminated her room. She rolled over and found Garick sitting on a chair by the window. He was staring out at their lands.

"Garick?"

He turned at the sound of her voice and smiled. Nell was sure, even in her sleepy state, that she saw fear behind his eyes.

"Today," he said.

He stood, nodded and left her room.

She stared at the foot of the bed. Foreign clothes were spread atop the blankets and odd-looking slippers sat on the floor. A huge grin crept across her face and excitement wriggled through her veins.

He said today. Today!

She peeled off the blankets, glad that Garick had picked today for them to go into Paraan. Thinking back to when she had asked him to take her, she realized it had been over six moons ago. So much had been revealed to her since then, and she was grateful he had not given in to her impetuousness.

She stared into the mirror and picked up her comb. She had found it on the shelf one morning, about three moons earlier. She dragged it through her silky crimson hair, now nearly reaching her chin, and the curls bounced back up after escaping the comb.

She dressed carefully, for she was unsure about the new attire. The slippers were heavy and ugly, but she wore them anyway.

As she entered the kitchen, Garick was eating a fruit.

He was beaming. "By Saros, if you did not act so much like your father, I would swear you were your mother!"

She grinned at this, but then a look of uncertainty crossed her face. "The slippers are strange. They feel so heavy."

"Ah, they are called *'boots'*. Humans always wore them, but I do not know why. I find them clumsy."

She nodded in agreement.

Garick set down his fruit core. "Now, let me get a look at you."

He walked toward her and adjusted her tunic, pulling

the tie over to her right side. "A Human wears their tunic knot on the opposite side their sword hangs." He patted her pants, a sad expression on his face. "You look so much older. I suppose we should be on our way."

By the time their horses neared Paraan, Nell began to feel the weight of her sword. "Garick, I never had to carry this before. Why must I now?"

"Well, you did not look Human before. Not only can it be unsafe to travel without a weapon, but it also shows who you are. Humans are known for their skill with a sword." He grinned. "And you certainly are no exception."

As they rode, Nell smiled at her new image. Her hair blew in the wind, the sensation sending her visions of her mother's plump red curls. The new clothes were less constricting, since the tunic folded over the outfit, unlike the traditional Elvish wrap. The pants almost had a mind of their own. They flowed around her skin like a soft breeze and were certainly a change from the skirt she had always worn.

They arrived in the village and passed a Dwarven baker cooling her fresh bread and an Elvish tailor arguing with a patron. Shocked eyes fell upon Nell, and many regarded her with looks of hatred. The village's busy sounds dwindled to nothing more than gossip mongering whispers. Soon, the clopping of the horses' hooves were the loudest noises heard.

Nell looked at Garick with sad, confused eyes.

"Pay no attention to it, Nell," he said. "These people have not seen a Human in many cycles. A lot of them think that by you being here, the Garshu will come. That is why they look at you like that. They do not know what to say or expect."

They drew to a halt at the bookshoppe and dismounted.

It seemed like the whole town watched them enter the store. Once inside, she breathed a sigh of relief. She turned and immediately became the one that stared.

A Sarkian couple owned the bookshoppe. It made sense to her now on why Garick had never let her in the bookshoppe before—the Sarkians would have recognized that she was Human no matter what disguise she wore. Nell had never seen Sarkians before and now they stood in front of her, by the door. The male was quite plain to look at, but his wife—as female Sarkians usually are—was unbelievably stunning. Her long dark hair shimmered purple in the sunlight that flooded the shop. She looked short for a Sarkian, maybe only seven feet tall. She was wearing a long dress made of a flowing material that Nell had never seen before. In the Sarkian manner, it was low-cut and very sensual.

It was well known that Sarkians' eye colours change with their moods. This Sarkian's eyes were a calm blue at that moment, but as she approached Nell, they changed to an orange colour. Orange represented happiness for a Sarkian.

"It is lovely to see you, Human." Her voice was deep yet gentle. "It has been a long time since one of your kind has come to Paraan. What is your title?"

Nell smiled timidly. "I am Nelhua. Please call me Nell."

"I am Anay."

She was careful not to shake Anay's hand, for she remembered that Sarkians abhorred physical contact. "I am looking for a book on Humans."

Anay nodded and led her to the corner of the shop. She left Nell to her perusal and headed back to speak with Garick.

Nell was pleased to be surrounded by such a vast selection of books. She pulled out the first one she saw that she did not recognize from their collection at home. Then she read the cover.

Humans – The Doomed Creatures
Details on Their Difficult Survival and
Eventual Extinction
By: Easrilar Suttendon

She judged by its immaculate condition that it had been recently published. Sarkians keep their belongings in pristine order, so she checked for a date inside. It was handwritten in the upper left corner, inside the heavy red cover.

Completed in the 34th age of Saros

So, it had been published recently. She sat down at the nearby table and opened the book.

The Origins of the Races
Once life in our world was established, the Goddess
Saros created eight races to replace the eight children
she lost in the God Wars (see reference 7), but was
unable to bear, due to her new form as Goddess.
Sarkians were the first, formed in the glorious image of
Saros' own Goddess. Dragons were next, created for
their might and strength. Then came Merfolk, to care for
the seas. Giants followed, their size and simple ways
delighting Saros. Humans after that, created in her
image and for their skill. Dwarves proceeded then,
endearing in their simplicity and caring for the physical
world. Elves next, pleasing Saros with their talents.
Garshu were created last, fashioned to toil for their
predecessors.

The last line surprised Nell. Apparently, Saros had always intended the Garshu to be slaves. They were never supposed to be otherwise.

No wonder they hold such a grudge.

She looked up from the book. Garick was watching her from the front of the store, peering at her repeatedly. His eyes looked over the top of the book he was holding upside down and pretending to read.

Only Garick would watch over me that intently.

She waved, arching a brow teasingly.

Garick gave a sheepish nod, then turned his book right side up.

Nell focused on the book in her hands.

The Anger Begins

When the Garshu began to cover the earth, they appointed a leader to help thrust off the shackles their race was destined to bear. His name was Opeart. He led the Garshu in an uprising, killing many. The Humans, blessed with the most skill for fighting, took the reins and led in opposing the Garshu. When a Human female named Bethecca was victorious in assassinating Opeart, his second—a vicious Garshulan named Etak—changed the Garshu's concentration. They decided to wipe out the entire Human race as a show of their power, and to avenge the death of Opeart. They brutally slaughtered the Human leader, and the war began. Many Garshu leaders have come and gone now, due to the exceptional threat a Human poses while grasping a blade.

Stunned by this new knowledge, she finished reading the selection. The Garshu were so barbaric, she was glad she only had fleeting memories of them.

Flipping a few pages further, she stopped.

A frown crossed her face, as she gazed down at a sketching with the caption: *Massacre at Merrill Shrine.* The drawing illustrated a field painted red with Human blood. There had to have been more than a thousand Human bodies—limbs and beheaded corpses.

She covered her now gaping mouth, her hand quivering.

"It is awful, is it not?"

She raised her head and found the Sarkian woman standing beside her, holding out a handkerchief. She took it and dried her eyes.

"I cannot believe such a thing could happen," she said.

Anay sat down beside her. "It makes you all the more special. There are not as many Humans left in Cantro, and that is exciting and daunting at the same time."

She stared at the page that Nell had been reading.

"I remember when this horrible event occurred." She looked directly at Nell, her eyes changing to a sad yellow. "And I will tell you…this picture makes the actual incident look far less brutal than it really was."

Chapter Six

Garick and Nell rode back to the cottage in silence.

Nell's horse was weighed down with the heavy volume that Anay had sold to her for a bargain. Garick did not mind purchasing it. He had seen Nell's face when she looked through parts of the book, and he knew she needed to have it.

"That one will make a proud addition to our little library, I think" he said finally.

"Aye."

"Ah, cheer up, little one. What say we do a little swordplay when we get back?"

"Aye," she answered, distracted by a strange feeling.

Her gaze swept further down the road.

"Stop!" she hissed.

Her head swivelled from side to side, searching. Closing her eyes for a moment, she listened.

At last, she looked at the Elf. "Someone is coming."

Garick peered down the road, his eyes straining.

"Move!" he ordered.

They pulled off to the side of the road and hid behind a cluster of trees. Nell noticed Garick had his bow drawn, and without even realizing it, she had extracted her sword.

They waited.

Soon, they heard the sound of horses.

Nell peered through the trees. She could see the

hooves of several horses, but the lush branches made it difficult to see the riders.

"Can you see them?" she whispered.

Garick nodded, looking worried.

Slowly, a head came into view, its grey ears and revolting black hair unmistakably expressing its identity.

Nell recoiled. *Garshu!*

The riders suddenly slowed as the leader signalled a silent warning.

Garick frowned and lowered his bow. "Something is not right."

They emerged from the trees once the troop had passed them. Nell could see the retreating backs of six Garshu. Frowning, she realized that Garick was right. In all the sketches she had seen of the Garshu, this group was very different.

"They sensed our presence," Garick told her. "The Garshu cannot do that."

He knocked his bow and shot a whistling arrow at the tree that the lead Garshulan was passing. The riders instantly split up, each taking cover. The metallic sound of swords being drawn filled the air, and the lead rider turned to face Garick, who fearlessly approached them.

He aimed his blade at Garick. "Who dares to strike?"

Garick lowered his bow. "Sir, I was just curious as to who would be brave enough to ride openly wearing the skin of a Garshulan."

Mouth gaping, Nell looked from Garick to the rider. Yes, now she realized why the creature looked so different.

Someone's face was underneath the Garshulan's.

The rider raised a hand and pulled back the fleshy mask. It fell onto his shoulders like a hood, revealing blonde locks and a masculine Human face.

Nell's jaw dropped even further.

"Why, a pack of Humans!" Garick exclaimed, his eyes wide with disbelief. "You do not know how rare and wonderful this is." Extending a hand, he stepped forward, an enormous grin upon his face. "I am Garick."

The Human shook his hand. "I am Liam. You surprised us with your shot." He gestured to the arrow sticking out of the tree.

"I apologize. One can never be too careful."

Garick strode to the tree and yanked the arrow from it.

A pair of brown eyes watched from behind the tree.

Garick smiled. "Hello, young lady."

A woman stepped forward, never taking her eyes off him.

"Be at ease, Lachlin." Liam said. "I don't believe he means us any harm."

At this, the four remaining riders materialized from their hiding places. Two more men—one young and one old—crept out from behind some bushes. An older woman appeared next, followed by a male child whose face and hands were covered in a web of spidery scars. He could not have been more than twelve.

Liam's arm swept the air. "This is my family, Elf. We've been in hiding for many cycles and are always on the go. I don't expect you to understand. You're not being hunted." His eyes were laced with loathing.

Nell immediately jumped from her hiding place. "Never again shall you speak to him like that. Garick has known fear in a way you could never comprehend." Her sword was in her hand, glinting in the afternoon sun.

Garick held up a hand. "Nell, please meet Liam. This is his family." He turned to Liam. "Sir, I would like you to meet *my* family. Her name is Nelhua. And as you can see, she is also one of the hunted."

Garick invited Liam and his kin back to their cottage for dinner. Liam had insisted against it, due to the threat they posed by being there. However, the Elf managed to convince him to come.

Nell had not said a word, since most of the group had not taken their eyes off her.

"This is our home," Garick said as they rode closer to the farm.

Liam surveyed the cottage and the lands.

"How do you live in the open like this? Don't the Garshu come here looking for the girl?"

Garick shrugged. "I have raised Nell in secret and her existence has been well concealed. There have not been Humans in this area for many cycles, so there is no reason for the Garshu to come here." He looked at Liam. "Did the Garshu come to your village often?"

Liam stared off into the distance. "Only once. My village was left alone for so long that we believed—like you—that the Garshu didn't know about it. The whole community was slaughtered in one night. Except for me and Lachlin."

He closed his eyes, cringing. He could still hear the children screaming while they were stabbed and tortured.

"My parents had gone to the next town to trade for the week. My twin sister and I hid. Afterward, we ran to the next dwelling and found everyone dead. There were bodies all over town. When the Garshu neared our location, we had to lie among the dead until they passed. We stayed there for hours, covered in the blood and pieces of our friends, until the last Garshulan was gone. Our parents never returned, so all we could assume was that the Garshu had killed them too."

Liam pointed to the others. "That's Treyton over there. Kris and Peter took us in. And we picked up the little one, Bean, a few cycles back." He motioned to the young boy. "We saved him from a fire. Garshu trapped him in a hut, lit it and left him to die. He wasn't yet six cycles of age."

Garick snuck a glance at the young boy, who was curiously watching Nell's every move. She seemed oblivious to Bean's ogling.

However, Nell was well aware of Treyton's constant gaze. She had never seen a Human male before. She had only seen them in books. Each time she tried to steal a look at him, she found Treyton already watching her. Frustrated, she decided to examine the other young male in their party.

Liam had shoulder-length blond hair and held himself very erect in his saddle. He looked around attentively, even while he spoke with Garick.

Nell looked at the sturdy old woman who was riding beside the older man. She was softly snoring, and her head bobbed with the bounce of the horse as she slept. Wisps of her silver hair escaped their loose bind. The old man next to her was missing his right hand and only the nub of his wrist was bared. He was stout, and strong. His long silver hair swept back with the breeze, revealing a dark scar across his right cheek. His face was weathered and Nell could tell he was a man who had seen interesting days.

The group reached the cottage.

Leading the horses to the stable, Nell turned to Liam. "Our barn will not hold all the horses, so Garick's, mine and two of yours must sleep outdoors tonight."

He nodded, motioning to Lachlin and Bean. They dismounted and wrapped their horses' straps to the railing.

Once inside, Garick showed them to the dining room and introduced his homemade thistonberry wine to the group. It was greatly welcomed.

Nell headed into the kitchen and began boiling water for dinner. She was cutting vegetables when Liam entered.

"It was very nice of you both to invite us to your home," he began, sitting on a seat carved from a tree stump.

"Aye, Garick is very sweet," she replied gruffly.

"Well, it's your home as well, is it not?"

Her eyes bore through him. "Garick invited you. Not I."

He stood, offended. "Why are you so curt with me? Have I wronged you in some way?"

Nell did not know what to say. She was not certain why she was so defensive of Garick, or so hostile toward Liam. She was not certain of any of the feelings she had when she looked at him.

When she did not answer, Liam stormed from the room. Shortly afterward, the old woman entered. Her eyes held the sparkle of a hundred constellations.

She approached Nell, a tentative smile on her face. "Dear, may I help you?" Her voice was sweet and gentle. "It's been so long since we've had a homemade meal, I just cannot sit and watch."

"Of course," Nell grinned. "Garick is with the others, so the help will be enormously welcomed."

She handed the elderly woman an apron and they set to work, kneading the fresh dough and preparing it for the oven. Nell began cooking a stew, while the woman tenderized a side of lamb.

After a while, Nell paused and faced the woman. "I just realized I do not know your name."

The woman smiled, wiping her hands on the apron. "My given name is Karistaal Elaina Coresani. They call me Kris, and you can too, if you like."

Nell nodded and resumed her work. It was strange yet nice to have another woman around, especially since she never had before.

"How long have you lived here?" Karistaal inquired.

"For as long as I can remember." Nell looked down at the flour-speckled floor. "I lived with my parents in another village, but when I was three they were murdered by the Garshu. Garick took me in, brought me here and raised me as an Elf. I was just told the truth about my family. And the truth about my race."

"I'm so sorry." Karistaal's expression proved she was genuine in her sympathy. "The Garshu raids on villages are awful."

"Oh, they did not attack the whole village," Nell said. "Just us…" She trailed off, suddenly perplexed. "I wonder why they came after only *us*. I never did ask Garick."

"Our own children were taken from us too."

Nell's heart ached when she heard this. "That is terrible. I cannot imagine a mother losing her children. I know I miss my parents. I wish I could remember them more."

"What happened?"

Nell relayed the entire appalling tale and Karistaal had a renewed respect after hearing it.

"Your family was very brave and strong." Karistaal closed her eyes. "Who were they, so I can put names to the heroic faces of these people in my mind?"

"Coada was my father and my mother was Illedria."

Karistaal gasped, her eyes flaring. "What?"

Nell frowned. "Coada and Illedria. They were my parents' names."

The old woman seemed stunned by this revelation.

Nell placed a hand on her arm. "Are you all right? Is something wrong?"

Karistaal shook off whatever had overcome her and took Nell's hand. "I-I'm fine. I just had a spell. I'm fine. Really."

"Just to be safe, please sit for a moment and tell me a story?" Nell smiled. "I love a good fable."

They gabbed away, to Nell's delight, while finishing the food. And nothing more was mentioned about her parents.

The men and Lachlin were seated in the dining area, sharing in Garick's wine.

"We need to attack!" Treyton pounded the table. "We can't sit idly by any longer while the Garshu cover this world like insects. We must fight back!"

Liam signalled him to calm. "I told you not to bring this up again. You know where we stand. We can't just assault the Garshu. They are too many. You know there are only a handful of Humans left in existence. Even finding Nell was a highly unusual occurrence. We're very likely the last."

At this, Nell and Karistaal entered with food. They set down what they were carrying and went back for the rest while Garick refilled the glasses and lit some candles. Darkness had begun to creep into the hall as the sun set to the south.

After the women returned, everyone took their seat and Garick led them in a brief prayer to Saros. Then they dug into the food.

To Nell's surprise, the old man spoke first, his voice husky, yet calming. "They call me Peter. I'd like to thank you both for extending us this invitation. I can't remember the last time we all slept indoors." He smiled, his mouth full.

The rest of the group grunted in gratitude.

"It has been a long time since we've had a nice meal like this," Treyton said. "Who knows when the next one will be, if we continue running." He looked directly at Liam.

"Forget that nonsense," Liam hissed.

"What nonsense?" Nell asked.

"Trey thinks we should all go throw our necks on a Garshulan blade," Liam replied sarcastically.

"Nay, I *don't!*" Treyton roared, rising from his chair. "I'm tired of running. I wish to avenge my family. It's been many, many cycles, Liam. I need to relieve that pain." He paced around the room. "The Garshu's desire for bloodshed has surpassed all logic. They are attacking Elf, Dwarven, and even Giant settlements. The population has had *enough*. We could begin a resistance; lead the people once again, like in the stories. Fight back!"

"Stop!" Liam bellowed. "You're living in the past. In a forgotten dream world. No one will fight. No one will follow us. And no one would oppose the Garshu."

"I would."

Nell's quiet voice instantly stilled the room.

Chapter Seven

Garick's head whipped around. "You will not talk of such things, Nell."

"I want to stand up for my race. I could do it."

"You will not! You will stay here, safe and far away from the nonsensical wars of the world."

"Garick," Treyton interjected, "this war will not stay away for long. The Garshu are enveloping us, and if she wishes to go into battle, perhaps you should consider it."

"She has the bloodline for it," Karistaal added. "Her parents were—"

"Stop!" Garick roared. "All of you! You are guests in my home and will not disrespect me by trying to send my only kin to her death." He stomped from the hall, leaving the room thick with tension.

Nell turned. "Karistaal, my parents were fishermen. Sure, they were good with a sword, but most Humans are."

"Your parents weren't like most Humans," Karistaal said.

The entire group looked at her, their expressions urging her to explain.

"All Humans are gifted with a blade, but your parents were...special," she said. "They had extraordinary skill, absolutely magnificent. Your parents were known far and wide. That is probably why the Garshu hunted them so fervently." She turned to the others. "Her parents were Coada and Illedria."

A collective gasp echoed in the air.

Garick suddenly burst into the room. "I do not want to leave Nell here with you all. You will fill her head with unsuitable ide—" He broke off, noticing that they were all staring at Nell in the strangest way. "What is going on?"

"I guess they have heard of my parents, Garick." Nell gestured toward the gaping mouths.

Liam cleared his throat. "You never told her about her parents' identity, Elf?"

Nell gazed at Garick in bewilderment. The Elf squeezed his eyes shut, as though trying to stifle a nightmare.

"Garick?" she murmured.

Her guardian sat down beside her.

"Nell, everything I told you about your parents is true. However, there is more to the tale. I neglected to divulge it because I did not want you running off to war." He glared at Liam. "Your mother Illedria was known to all. Legend has it that she was a descendant of the Goddess Saros—or rather a direct descendant of the initial Human, Shirell, who was created by Saros. Now this is only legend. There is no longer any evidence. Families kept records of their lineage and added to it as life expanded. When the Garshu destroyed your parents' home, the documentation burned as well. Many believed your mother to be Shirell's last true heir. With you being Illedria's only child, that would make you the heir."

Treyton leapt from his chair. "Can't you see that this is a sign? Shirell's last daughter has been delivered to us. She'll save us all."

"No!" Garick snapped. "She will not save anyone. She is just a child."

"She's old enough," Treyton argued.

"I say she is *not!*"

"Quiet!" Nell's face was red with fury. "You discuss me as though I were not here." She faced them, furious. "In your opinion, I may not be old enough to fight. However, I am most definitely old enough to speak for myself. You will sit down and Garick will finish the story."

Treyton obeyed, red-faced.

"Garick," Nell said. "Please continue."

The Elf nodded. "Now then, you know about your mother. Your father's tale is not quite so dramatic. He was born into a poor fishing family and was raised doing just that. When he was fifteen, he claimed a messenger from Saros spoke to him one day while out on the water. Coada said the messenger told him to travel to a small village on the other side of Cantro to find his fortune. Despite the objections of his kin, he listened to his intuition and went in search of riches. He found not jewels and currency, but the most beautiful woman he had ever seen—Illedria. Coada brought her back to his family and they were wed. Some say the essence of Shirell attended that day. As it turned out, Illedria was quite wealthy and her kin showered them with gifts. They lived in a cottage near Coada's relatives, on the outskirts of the village Hhasta. Eventually, they had a lovely little girl they named Nelhua. They were very happy." His smile quickly diminished. "The rest of the story you know."

Everyone was quiet for some time.

Then Karistaal broke the silence. "Aye, it's time for everybody to be going to sleep. We have an early start."

"Oh no," Nell objected. "You cannot leave tomorrow. You must stay a little longer."

"We'll see in the morning," Liam said firmly.

The group dispersed and Garick directed each person to their spot for the night. Bean was the smallest, so he was given a cozy corner on some hay. Lachlin and Karistaal were given Nell's bed, while she slept on the floor in the room. Peter reluctantly took Garick's bed, with Treyton sleeping on the floor nearby. Meanwhile, Garick made a bed in a corner in the kitchen, on sacks of wheat. Liam asked for a spot in front of the hearth in the centre of the cottage, where it was possible to watch all corners of the home. He told Garick it was because it was the warmest spot.

Everyone knew different.

Lachlin was the last to wake the next morning. She looked around and saw she was alone in Nell's room. She cursed as she leapt out of bed.

As she changed into her day clothes, she noticed a sketching on the shelf. She took a closer look.

The woman in it was beautiful. She looked like Nell, but with longer hair and a slightly different smile.

"It must be her mother," Lachlin murmured.

Compelled, she reached out to touch the sketching before realizing her mistake.

She had forgotten to don her gloves.

She was instantly swept away to a pulsating vision. She lay on the ground, staring at a sapphire sky. She tried to sit up, but found she could not, for her belly was enlarged with child.

In the distance, she heard swords clashing. And screams. Then nothing.

Suddenly, Lachlin heard a faint voice.

"You must go."

A massive explosion rattled the air and flames licked the skies to her left.

"NO!" she screamed.

Her head slammed into the ground. Her vision swam.

As several Garshu approached, she fought a wave of unconsciousness.

A Garshulan nudged her with his metal boot.

"Thand wantsss thisss one alive. Grab her and throw her in the cart."

A clawed hand reached for her.

Then everything went black.

At the vision's abrupt end, Lachlin stumbled back onto the bed, whimpering in pain and biting back tears. She rubbed her legs. She could still feel the numbness. With shaking hands, she pulled on her gloves, vexed that she had even taken them off the night before. She ran a shaky hand over her flat stomach, still feeling the life within from the vision.

"I haven't had a vision like that in many moons."

Composing herself, she headed to the hall. Finding no one there, she stuck her head into the room in which Peter and Treyton were sleeping.

Empty.

She proceeded to the kitchen where she found everyone huddled around the window facing the field.

"Thanks for waking me," Lachlin muttered, jabbing Liam in the ribs.

Her brother motioned to the field. "Look at this."

Outside, Nell and Garick were sword fighting, and it was blatant who was winning. They grunted as their swords met, yet neither could push through to the other.

"Break!" Garick ordered.

They broke apart, breathing heavily.

"Again!" Nell commanded after a moment's rest.

They each took a starting position. Then Garick stepped forward, bringing his sword down toward her head. She swiftly blocked and whirled around, ending up underneath him. She poked him in the abdomen with the hilt of her sword.

Then she looked at him and winked. "Gotcha."

The two disengaged and took a new starting pose.

Nell raised her eyebrows for a moment, challenging her guardian. He ran at her, his sword slashing in quick diagonal waves. She blocked the first hit, but did not anticipate his prompt relocation of the blade next to her hip. She just barely prevented his connection, reacting just as hastily with a strike at his arm. She halted the blade only a touch from him.

Garick stared at the sword, surprised.

Nell smiled.

Unable to catch his breath, Garick spoke between gasps.

"I cannot believe...how quickly...you have...caught on."

She laughed. "Other Humans are the same, I am sure."

When he did not answer, she said, "Again?"

"Liam, I must speak with you," Lachlin whispered, wringing her gloved hands.

"Just a moment," he answered, his eyes still fixed on Nell's swift movements.

"Liam, please!"

Lachlin tugged on his arm and he snapped out of his trance-like state.

"Aye, what is it?"

"Let's go into another room, brother."

Mesmerized by the scene outside, Liam reluctantly pulled away from the window.

"Looks like Garick finally has the upper hand," he said.

Lachlin gave him a strange look. "For the moment."

"Do you surrender?" Garick arrogantly asked Nell.

He was standing over her, their swords meeting above her head as she crouched on one knee.

She glanced to his right.

Falling for her diversion, he turned.

Too late.

Nell pushed him off.

He twisted when she swung at him, and his head whipped around just in time to block her blow.

They veered back and forth, circling and repeatedly attacking, never quite completing a strike. They moved from side-to-side so quickly, they became a blur to anyone who watched them.

Liam led Lachlin to a seat in the hall.

"Now, what's so urgent?" he asked, distracted.

"I've had a vision."

At that, he focused his attention on his sister. "When?"

"Just earlier, in the room where I slept. I didn't wear my gloves to bed, and before I was even fully awake, I touched a picture. Of Nell's mother. I-I touched it and saw the day that Nell believes her mother was killed. Only...she wasn't killed."

Liam gaped at her, but remained silent.

"What Nell doesn't know," she continued, "is that her mother was taken captive. And she was with *child*. Saros only knows if that poor baby died a decent death. And Nell's mother...they could've tortured her for quite some time." She eyed him, uncertain. "Should we tell her?"

"No, absolutely not," Liam said quickly. "It would only upset her. We'll keep this between us for now." He leaned forward and took his sister's gloved hands. "Now, are *you* all right? I know what these visions can do to you. And this one sounds especially hard."

"I'm fine. A bit shaken. It just makes me wish I could be like other Humans and have normal visions. Others get to just observe, while I'm forced to relive what I see. It doesn't seem fair."

They headed back into the kitchen.

Nell entered shortly afterward.

"I ain't never seen anyone move like that," Bean blurted in awe. "You're incredible with that sword."

"Aye, you've some talent there, girl," Peter agreed.

Garick joined them, a look of resignation on his face. He carried a slender, heavy object wrapped in a blanket.

"Nell, I have been waiting thirteen cycles to give this to you." He solemnly presented her the object, then stepped back. "I believe you earned it today."

The kitchen grew quiet.

Unwrapping the gift, Nell gasped.

"Do you know what that is?" Garick asked.

"Aye, I do."

With tears rimming her eyes, Nell held her mother's

sword for everyone to see. It almost sang out as she wielded it, and she seemed to grow at that moment, her very presence filling the cottage.

She turned to Garick. "Where has this been?"

"I had it in my closet. I found it half buried the day your parents died."

"By Saros, what else do you have in there?"

Garick winked. "Ah, do not concern yourself about that." His eyes swept across the room. "Since we are all awake, is anyone hungry?"

He was answered with enthusiastic nods.

"Nell and I will make some breakfast," he said. "After, we will talk."

He looked directly at Liam and Treyton.

Chapter Eight

Clearing the dishes from a delicious breakfast of eggs, bacon and fruit, Nell walked into the kitchen and grabbed a fresh pitcher of juice. She returned to the dining hall and poured everyone a glass.

A discussion was already underway.

"Garick, the family and I have discussed it," Liam announced. "And although we're torn about some things, we do know this. We'd love for you and Nell to join us."

Nell looked at Garick in surprise.

He greeted her with the same look.

"We think all Humans should stay together," Liam continued. "Separating after we now know that each other exists would be folly. What do you say?"

Garick took a breath. "Liam, as wonderful as it is to be with all of you, Nell and I cannot leave our home. Why could you not all just stay here?"

Liam's mouth thinned. "I know you think the Garshu will stay away forever, but we must keep moving. We need to survive. That's what's important."

"Why not look at things this way," Treyton interjected. "If we instigated a rebellion against the Garshu, we could defeat them and come back here to live in peace. We could do it." His eyes desperately searched for agreement.

"I'll never forget the face of the dying Garshulan who

gnawed my hand off," Peter said, staring at his missing hand. "I couldn't even stop him. I lay there after the battle with both my legs broken and I just let him die with my hand in his mouth. I was sure I would die as well. Only Saros knew I would awake to one of her angels."

He looked at Karistaal and caressed her cheek. "I'm tired of running. I agree with Treyton, in that we need to fight back. Even if we do survive for cycles and cycles, the Garshu will only come for our children. It needs to stop."

Silence followed his statement. It lasted for a few minutes, as everyone tended to his or her opinions.

Nell had not thought of the situation that way, and she did not know if she could fight.

"Why don't we spend today and tonight here?" Lachlin's crystal voice broke in. "Let everyone think about what they want to do. I think we all need some time."

Lachlin sat outside the cottage, listening to the night air. She was nibbling on a chunk of bread when Nell arrived from the fields. She motioned for Nell to sit down in the cool grass.

"I hope that whatever is decided," Nell said with a smile, "we all stay together. Not that Garick is not great, it is just that having other women here is…even greater."

Lachlin's gaze drifted away.

The day had been lovely, with everyone pitching in on chores. Later, they had spent time reading and playing games.

Except for Liam.

He stayed by the window or skulked outside, watching the horizon for signs of unwelcome visitors.

"What?" Nell asked, interrupting her thoughts.

"You're always so happy." Lachlin gave a soft sigh, and then faced her. "Doesn't it bother you that our small band here is probably the last in Cantro? We must always be one step ahead of the Garshu."

She lay back on the grass, her arms behind her head.

"Treyton wants us to face the Garshu and fight back, but Liam will never allow it. Sometimes I want to, just to have the chance to get a Garshulan myself. For our mother. She had the most beautiful hair. I remember it was gold, like the sun emanated from it. And our father? He was so strong, the way Liam is. Alas, I know we wouldn't have a hope of winning. They'd slaughter us all."

Nell stretched out beside her and her eyes wandered to Lachlin's scarred neck. She frowned, trying to make out the odd mark. Before she could say anything, Lachlin pulled up her shift to cover her neck.

"Treyton is even more determined after meeting you," Lachlin said softly. "He believes your lineage is a sign from Saros—that we were destined to meet you. He thinks you're here to save us all. What do you think?" She looked into Nell's eyes.

"I think I need to sleep. Good night."

Nell headed for the cottage.

Lachlin stared at the stars.

"I think it's time for you to wake up."

Nell felt a bit of a chill when she entered the cottage. Shivering, she moved toward the fire that crackled in the dining hall. She sat on the hand-woven rug and took in the heat.

She had held back her feelings from Lachlin. She wanted to rebel with Treyton, but she was not ready to kill Garshu by the thousands. She wanted to stand up for her race and all the others that the Garshu had hurt. Her instincts told her it was something she *had* to do.

"Here," a voice behind her said.

She looked over her shoulder.

"Hot cider," Liam said, offering her a cup.

Grateful, she took it. "Thank you."

He slumped in the chair beside her and stared into the fire. "Treyton has been gone since morning. We had an argument and he said he was going to prove his point."

His words were slurred.

"I can't help but feel like he is partially right," he said. "I know I don't want to put my family in danger, but I agree with him and Peter. If we don't do something, this will never end."

Nell felt his burning eyes caress her face.

"You know," he mumbled. "You have beautiful skin."

She blushed. Then, suspicious, she sniffed his mug.

"Liam, you're drunk!"

He blinked. "I'm not drunk. I've only had a few cups of cider."

"There is no cider in there. There is only wine."

When she said this, Liam flicked a look at his cup, then tilted his head and threw back the last of it.

"Well, I'm not saying this because of the wine. You *are* beautiful." He shifted closer. "I think Treyton is right that we should fight back. However, I'm afraid. Me of all people, afraid of losing the people I love most. But do you know why I think we could win?" His face was dangerously close. "You."

"Liam—"

"Do you not see?" He touched her cheek. "You're my inspiration. With you here, we could do anything. *I* could do anything."

His face drew near and he kissed her. His lips were warm, gentle. Nell's mind dissolved when she realized that it was her first kiss. And it was…awkward.

A shadow suddenly poured over them.

Pulling away, Nell saw Treyton standing in the doorway. A sad look adorned his face as he turned and briskly walked away.

The cottage door slammed.

Liam staggered out the door. "Treyton!"

In the hall, Nell watched him go, her mind reeling.

Karistaal was awake early the next morning. As she strolled outside, her hands brushed the ivy that crawled up the side of the cottage. She veered around the corner and nearly tripped over Treyton. He was curled up in the grass. She tried to walk around, so as not to wake him.

"It's no use trying to tiptoe," Treyton mumbled, his eyes still shut. "I heard you almost fall on me."

Karistaal crouched down next to him. "Why are you sleeping out here? You should take advantage of a bed while you have one. Who knows how long we'll be here."

"Kris, you have been like a mother to me, ever since I lost mine. Can I ask you something?"

She nodded.

"Aren't I fair? Pleasing to the eye of a woman?"

Karistaal's eyebrows arched. "Are you referring to the lovely Nelhua? Do you fancy her?"

"No, it's not...it has nothing to do with...anyone here," he stammered. "I-I just was thinking about it. We are always so busy defending ourselves and always on the move, I guess being left to my thoughts in such a carefree place got the best of me." He stood abruptly. "Forget I asked. It was stupid."

He disappeared inside the cottage.

Karistaal shook her head, knowing the truth behind his questions.

Poor lad.

Treyton headed for the kitchen.

Why do I even care about that stupid kiss? It's none of my business. Focus on today. I didn't go to all that hard work yesterday for it to be abandoned.

Nell peeked up from the breakfast she was making when he entered the kitchen. He tried to smile.

Absolutely nothing is wrong.

"G'morning, Nell. It smells great."

Nell said nothing. She watched Treyton vanish into Garick's room, where he should have slept, but had not.

With a shrug, she went back to chopping fruit.

Soon, a heated discussion emanated from Garick's room.

She dried her hands and approached the door, but it burst open and Garick stalked past her.

"We are going into town today," he said. "Something is happening."

Liam followed close behind.

Nell wanted to kick herself for blushing at the sight of the young man, but Liam did not even acknowledge her presence. Instead, he stormed out the cottage door.

She peered into Garick's room.

Treyton was staring out the window.

"What is going on?" she asked.

"I'm going to prove my point today." He faced her, his eyes ablaze. "I hope you're ready for a war."

When everyone had mounted their horses, they headed into town. Nell rode tall, leading the group. She experienced a sense of pride that she had not felt before. She was riding with those of her race. It was a wonderful feeling.

As they entered the village, they passed groups of Dwarves flocking to the inn, each Dwarf trying to crowd inside for a drink. All along the fences, there were more horses tied than normal. There were even several Neeshan Troffers secured to large boulders. The closest Troffer tossed its shaggy head and roared at the insects that bothered it.

Nell stared at them, greatly surprised.

Troffers were huge creatures—as tall as a cottage. They had drooling noses. Luckily, they did not stink, although their flabby, unkempt appearance would suggest otherwise.

Garick leaned toward her. "There must be Giants in town today. That is unusual."

Passing the bookshoppe, Nell saw the Sarkians inside greeting fellow members of their race.

"Is there some sort of anniversary today that I am unaware of, Garick? Why are all these people here?"

Her guardian shrugged. "All Treyton told me was there

would be some sort of gathering against the Garshu."

When they reached the town square, Nell saw hordes of people gathered as if waiting for something.

Or someone.

Karistaal and Peter dismounted and tied their horses, while Liam and Lachlin rode around a bit more to inspect the situation. With all the excitement, the group's arrival had gone unnoticed—until Treyton rode up onto a platform.

Whispers of anticipation rippled through the crowd.

"Fellow Cantronians, I am Treyton Bentley Kael. I come to you with a plea. There's a situation that has been brewing for many a cycle. Now it's affecting all of us. Our way of life—nay, our very *lives*—are threatened by the ongoing existence of the Garshu. They have killed our loved ones, destroyed our homes, and we have survived—left with nothing but bitterness and mourning."

"Aye!" someone shouted.

Grunts of agreement echoed in the air.

"Now, I don't know about you," Treyton said, "but I'm tired of running. I don't want to survive all these cycles only to have my children and their children hunted down."

The masses cheered, the sound deafening.

A Dwarf stepped forward, his eyes full of rage. "The Garshu 'ave left our village alone for many cycles, now that yer kind doesn't dwell nearby anymore. Why should I risk my life and my family's to fight a war that doesn't concern me?"

The fickle crowd roared in agreement.

Treyton raised a hand, silencing them.

"The Garshu may leave you alone now. Do you think they won't come for you once all Humans are dead? It has already begun. Why, there was a Garshu attack on a Giant settlement last moon."

Several Giants nodded.

"They want to destroy everyone and everything," he continued. "They haven't attacked your village because they just haven't gotten here yet."

Whispered discussions surged through the crowd.

An older Elf raised a tentative hand. "But how can we defeat them all? There are so many more of them. It would be impossible to win."

"Nothing is impossible," Liam cut in, joining Treyton on the platform. "If we all band together, we can form a plan—and a good one at that. Anyone willing to fight should meet us back at the square in one fortnight."

Murmurs filled the air, followed by applause.

The Giants sauntered over to their Troffers, loudly conversing with each other. Elves dispersed in many directions, most of them to their homes in the village. Dwarves hurriedly scattered, discussing the day's events in their throaty manner.

Liam grinned at Treyton, and they shook hands forcefully, pleased at the outcome.

"I told you I'd prove my point," Treyton said, smirking.

Nell watched as the crowd separated in a noisy bustle. She felt great happiness and dire fear at the same time. The idea of war sickened her.

As she surveyed the town, she noticed that a small group of visiting Sarkians had witnessed the meeting. None had said a word.

"I will be right back," she told Garick.

The Sarkians entered the shop and Nell quickly followed them inside. When they turned, they smiled at her. Anay, the Sarkian female who had assisted her before in the shop, moved gracefully toward her.

"Hello Nelhua, how lovely to see you again."

"Aye, hello," Nell replied. "I...er..."

She was suddenly overwhelmed by the Sarkians' surreal presence. They watched her, waiting, eyes a pleasant flaming orange.

"I apologize for my intrusion," she said. "I can come back at a more convenient time."

"No!" the Sarkians said in unison.

They ushered her to a seat and a Sarkian male brought

her a cup of hot Sark tea, while the Sarkian female sat next to her.

"Please, Nelhua," Anay urged. "What do you need?"

"I was just curious about the Sarkians' view on all of this. Are you willing to fight?" She took a sip of tea and waited.

"Sarkians do not join in the affairs of the rest of the world. We have always observed the issues from a distance, not participating, only cleaning up after everyone has finished their foolishness. There is no glory in death."

"But we need to take care of ourselves. If we do not do something, the Garshu will kill every Human. And anyone else in their way."

Anay smiled. "They could not kill *all* Humans."

Nell grew impatient. "Are you not aware that there are only a handful of us left?"

Shocked murmurs swept through the bookshoppe. The Sarkians looked at each other, their eyes widening and turning grey—the colour of concern.

"That cannot be true," Anay said, shaking her head. "We would be aware of such an atrocity. There have been many of your kind murdered, but surely there are more than a handful of you left?"

Nell's eyes stung. "I am sorry, Anay. But it is true."

Chapter Nine

A Sarkian male signalled everyone to quiet.

"I think we need to discuss a few things," he said. "I will contact Chrontan."

Nell recognized the name as the Sarkian leader. The man speaking must be his second, to be permitted to address him so casually.

She set her tea on the table. "I should be getting back. Thank you for the tea."

When she stepped outside, Garick was standing on the step. He had a clear view inside.

She playfully shoved him. "Not worrying, are we?"

"I always worry."

They walked back to the square where Bean and Lachlin were talking. Their conversation halted.

Bean looked at Nell, a troubled air about him.

"What is it?" she asked. "Where are Liam and Treyton?"

She followed Lachlin's eyes to the road out of town.

"They heard a rumour," Lachlin said, her eyes wide with alarm. "They've left to seek the truth. I don't know what was said, but I feel it's not good."

A feeling of trepidation grew in the pit of Nell's stomach. She instinctively reached for her sword. The cold metal of the hilt brought her comfort.

"From whom did they hear this gossip?" Garick asked.

"Peter and Kris said they overheard something," Bean

said. "They all went to speak with some folks in there."
He pointed to the inn that was flooded with Dwarves.
"Then Liam and Treyton left a few moments ago, but
Peter and Kris haven't come out yet."

Nell strode toward the inn, Garick in tow. She pushed
open the thick wooden doors and the stench of urine and
sweat filled her nostrils. Shuddering, she searched the
interior. She spotted Peter and Karistaal in the corner.
They were conversing with a young Dwarven woman
and an Elvish man.

Nell walked toward them, passing dozens of onlook-
ers who were drowning themselves in the dark ale that
the seedy barkeep was serving.

The Elf looked Garick up and down, his eyes narrow-
ing. Garick did not return the acknowledgement.

"What is going on?" Nell asked. "Where have Liam and
Treyton gone?"

The Dwarf eyed her warily. "An' who are ye?"

Despite her short stature, the woman's body was solid
and she emitted an air of inner strength.

"This is Nelhua," Karistaal said. "She's with us."

Peter turned to Garick. "These folks just arrived with
their tribes, traveling from the south. They say they have
spotted bands of Garshu raiding the small villages to the
east. Joilar has already been ransacked. The Garshu are
now heading to Follok. That would bring them here
tomorrow. We need to move. Now!"

"Perhaps they got wind of the rebellion," the Elf
suggested.

Garick shook his head. "No, if they had, they would
have traveled straight to Paraan and not stopped to
please themselves."

"Where did Liam and Treyton go?" Nell asked, worried.

Garick gave Peter a worried look. "Do they actually
expect to see the Garshu?"

Liam and Treyton rode their horses hard. Saros' Hill
was said to be one of the highest in Cantro. When they

reached the grassy peak, they leapt off their steeds.

"There!" Liam pointed to a trickle of black smoke bleeding upwards in the distance. "That's Joilar. The fires are still burning. The travelers were speaking the truth."

"That means the Garshu will be in Paraan by tomorrow," Treyton replied, squinting at the smoke.

"Could they know anything about the meeting?"

"I don't know how they could. I only informed the nearby communities. And what's more, they would not be stopping to burn small towns if they were coming to attack us."

Liam's mouth thinned. "Either way, we only have until tomorrow to get into hiding before they arrive."

Scanning the horizon one last time, they mounted their horses, then headed back.

By the time Liam and Treyton reached the outskirts of the village, the rest of their group were anxiously awaiting their return. Around them, the crowd of Elves, Dwarves and even Sarkians quickly doubled, then tripled. Word had gotten out about the approaching Garshu, and people were beginning to worry.

"What is going on?" an Elvish woman yelled, drawing her son near. "Are the Garshu actually coming here?"

Alarmed voices shouted their concern.

Liam drew a breath. "Yes."

A Dwarf broke through the crowd. "Curse ye foolish Humans. We 'ave had peace in this community for nigh on ten cycles. Yer wicked presence is causing this. In the name of Saros, *get out!*"

Slowly, a cry rippled through the crowd, until finally a thunderous roar filled the air.

"Silence!" Peter yelled.

But his voice was overpowered.

Nell vaulted onto her horse and cantered into the centre of the mob, but angry farmers and villagers shoved her, their emotions mounting.

"Stop!" she screamed. "This is not our fault! We must work together."

From the back of the mob, a hush began to spread.

Nell peered into the crowd and let out a gasp.

The Sarkians were silencing the townsfolk. A small group of them were slowly moving their arms in an arc over the gathering.

Nell tried again. "It is not our fault. The Garshu do not know of our presence here. They are coming here to do the same thing they are doing to every town. They will rob you and burn your homes. They will kill you if you try to stop them." She glared at the angry Dwarf. "They will kill you, even if you *do not* try. You are naive if you believe they will not harm you."

Frustrated, she raised her voice. "Do you see now how this affects you? They no longer hunt Humans because they think we are all gone. Now they are coming for *you*. For your homes. And for your children."

Many people in the crowd hugged their kin to them, realizing the truth in her words.

"What do we do?" an Elvish woman screamed.

Treyton manoeuvred his horse next to Nell's.

"There is not much you can do," he said. "If you have kin outside the village, stay with them until the Garshu have passed through. If you don't, find a safe place to hide and call upon Saros to grant us all good fortune. Try to stay calm and don't—"

"Garshu!" a voice bellowed. "They are coming *now!*"

Madness ensued as the townsfolk scattered to their homes, shrieking and crying.

"Saros help us!" Liam shouted.

His words were drowned out as the screams heightened.

The chaos spooked Nell's horse and it reared forcibly, throwing her into the air. She tensed, preparing for the impact of the hard, dusty ground. Instead, she hovered for a moment in mid-air, before landing in front of Treyton. On his horse.

Before she could utter a word, Treyton kicked his horse and they swiftly broke through the confused crowd. She looked back, but could not make out any familiar faces.

"We need to find a place to hide," Treyton shouted.

Nell pointed to the bookshoppe. "There! They will help us."

Quickly dismounting, they raced into the shop and skidded to a stop, surprised. The Sarkians were waiting for them. They had already pulled a bookcase from the wall.

"In here!" Anay urged.

Nell smiled briefly. "Thank you for participating this time."

Nell immediately sprinted to the bookcase, followed by Treyton. There was a small but adequate cavity behind it and they squeezed inside, while the Sarkians pushed the shelf back into place, throwing Nell and Treyton into near darkness.

The town grew deathly quiet.

Then Nell heard the Garshu riding into the village. She flinched when their heavy boots pounded the ground as they dismounted. Judging by the noise, there were at least twenty.

In the tight space, she twisted her arm until her fingers swept across the hilt of her sword. A familiar rush of relief poured over her and her mind immediately cleared.

She glanced at Treyton's indistinct form. His back was to her as he peeked through a crack in the bookcase.

"What about the others?" she whispered, panicked. "We have to make sure they're all right."

"Don't worry," he said. "They are more than capable of taking care of themselves. They're probably hiding somewhere, just like us."

Footsteps thumped by the front the shop.

"Quiet!" Anay warned.

After a long while, they heard nothing.

"Treyton, thank you for helping me back there," Nell whispered.

In the gloom, Treyton wedged his body around to face her. Their noses were only a finger's width apart.

"I have an idea I wanted to tell you and Liam about," she added. "I think we can defeat the Garshu. I have been thinking about it for awhile."

Treyton tried to control his breathing. He failed miserably. Nell's mere presence was intoxicating. Her eyes sparkled, despite the darkness. He watched her lips moving, hearing nothing. He gaped at her, until his stomach tightened and his mouth went dry.

"Treyton, what do you think?"

"I, um…sorry, what do I think of what?"

"My plan. Do you think it will work?"

"I…didn't quite catch it all. What was that last part?"

Nell gave him a puzzled look. "Are you okay?"

"Me? Oh yes, fine. I am fine. What was your plan?"

"I said…once we get to the caves, one of us could wipe out the females. After that, they will have no way to breed. Then we would only have to wipe out the armies."

Treyton stared at her as though she were insane.

"Do you know anything about the Garshulas?"

Nell looked away. "Not really."

"Garshulas aren't kept together," he explained. "If they see another female, they go mad. They're kept in different caves, just far enough from one another."

"So whoever goes in can kill them."

Treyton shook his head. "Even if we could pierce the nests, once a Garshula is in danger, the other one senses it and produces a female egg. It will never stop, Nell."

The sound of Garshu swords clanging in the distance emphasized his words.

"What if we planned a harmonized attack?" she said.

Treyton frowned. "I don't—"

"That could work," she interrupted, excited. "If you and I each attacked a Garshula at the same time, they would not have time to produce another female." She searched his face for approval.

"Good idea," he said, nodding. "In fact, it's brilliant. However, it's too dangerous for you. Liam and I will each take one."

Nell scowled. "No, I can do it."

"Look, you've just picked up the sword. You're not trained enough."

"Treyton, it was *my* idea."

"Keep your voice down!" he hissed. "It's a great idea, but you are not the one who will fulfill it. Understand that *now*. There are dangers in a Garshula nest that you cannot even imagine."

Nell stared at him defiantly. Or so she thought. In reality, she gave the appearance of a sulking child as she twisted away from him.

He rolled his eyes, annoyed.

She is such an infant. I don't know what I've been thinking.

But the sight of Nell's bare neck and the sugary scent of her newly grown hair gave him that familiar weak feeling in the pit of his stomach.

He closed his eyes, hoping to send it away.

Nell had an equally frustrated look on her face.

Treyton is so conceited. He knows that he and Liam are superior with a blade and he wants to flaunt it.

His words had left her feeling very insignificant. She realized she was new with a sword, but she needed to do something to aid them. And Saros help her, she *would*.

Chapter Ten

Hiding in a haystack, Lachlin watched in fear as the Garshulan leader swung down from his horse, stirring the dust with his loud landing. Several black legs joined him.

"Pathetic townssspeople," a jeering voice said. "Lisssten to what I am about to ssay. We have heard talk offf a band offf lawlesss Humansss. They are sssaid to have come through thisss way. Thessse Humansss will do nothing but sssteal fffrom you, and harm you. Tell usss which way they've gone and we will leave you all in peace."

The Garshulan sauntered toward a group of Elf children whose parents were nowhere in sight. He began caressing one young girl's face.

"Do not make usss do thingsss we need not do."

Lachlin eased back the hay and saw the old Dwarf, the one who had cursed them earlier. His beady eyes were staring directly at the haystack that concealed her.

"Aye, we 'ave seen these rogues," he admitted.

Lachlin held her breath.

As the Garshulan shuffled over to the Dwarf, an Elf jumped from behind and swiftly jabbed the Dwarf in the throat, rendering him silent as he slid to the ground.

"Oops!" the Elf exclaimed.

When he turned, Lachlin recognized him immediately.

"Garick!" she whispered.

"Do you wish thisss man not to speak, Elfff?" the

Garshulan asked.

Garick gave him a huge toothy grin. "Nay, it was an accident. I was coming over to hear better and my arm slipped."

The Garshulan's eyes narrowed. He strode over to the Elf girl, grabbing her fiercely by the neck.

"The throat isss sssuch a tender ssspot."

He lifted the girl into the air and she cried out as his filthy hand tightened around her neck.

The entire town stood frozen in unnatural stillness.

Garick took a step forward. "Hey, wait a—"

"No! You've inssspired me with your little...*accident.* I think you all know where thossse Humansss went. But you didn't want him to tell me." He gestured to the Dwarf lying on the ground.

Garick approached the Garshulan and the terrified child.

"I will tell you where they have gone if you put her down," he said.

The Garshulan stared vacantly. "I don't bargain, Elfff. I will do what I want."

"Put her down," Garick insisted. "Only then will I tell you what you want to know."

The Garshulan boiled over with anger. He grunted and tossed the child like a rag doll onto the ground. With swift strides, he stalked over to Garick and leaned down, their faces bare inches apart.

"You have robbed me offf the pleasssure offf ssslitting the childsss throat," he hissed. "Now tell me what you know. Or you both die."

Behind the Garshulan, the girl sat up. Then she stood, trembling.

"The Humans stopped here briefly for supplies," Garick said, hoping to distract the Garshulan. "Yesterday. They left around mealtime, in *that* direction." He pointed to the path that led to the village of Cholart.

Instantly, the Garshu mounted their horses.

The leader leaned down and pointed a sword at Garick.

"I had better not sssee you again, Elfff."

Garick's eyes were steely. "Aye, I am sure you will."

Infuriated by the Elf's answer, the Garshulan's gaze slid over to the little girl.

"No!" Garick yelled, racing toward the child.

The Garshulan kicked his horse into gear. When he passed by the Elf girl, he reared his sword, leaned over one side and brought the blade down upon her. A streak of blood glimmered on the blade as the Garshulan drew it back. Then he followed his army out of the village, setting alight a trail of cottages.

Garick reached the Elf girl and crouched next to her.

She was already dead.

Pale blue eyes stared blindly at the sky. Her slender throat had been sliced open and thick, red blood dripped onto the ground. Next to her lifeless body lay a broken doll.

Garick went numb at the sight.

Lachlin crawled out of the haystack and moved toward him.

"It *wasn't* your fault," she said in a quiet voice.

A group of villagers pushed past them. A sobbing Elvish woman—the girl's mother—crumpled to the ground next to the child's body.

Garick turned away, his mouth set in a grim line.

"Garick," Lachlin said. "You did everything—"

"There were too many people blocking the way for me to reach Nell," he muttered, changing the subject. "Did you see where she went?"

Lachlin shook her head. "All I saw was Treyton helping her out of the mob."

Garick grunted his disappointment.

Then they set off in search of their friends.

"Nelhua?" Anay called.

The bookcase was eased back, revealing two rather dusty Humans. Nell and Treyton sat back-to-back, arms crossed, stubborn expressions on their faces. Ignoring each other, they climbed from the cramped space.

Treyton nodded to the Sarkian woman. "Thank you for hiding us. If I could have chosen a different roommate, I might have enjoyed the stay."

"Funny," Nell snapped.

Moving away from him, she inclined her head to Anay. "I do appreciate what you did for us. Thank you."

She hastily departed the bookshoppe, with Treyton two strides behind. They slowed when they realized that they had no idea where to start looking for their friends.

"Where *is* everyone?" she murmured. "We hid in the bookshoppe so quickly, I did not get a chance to notice where anyone else went."

When they reached the fence, they discovered that the horses were grazing on a patch of grass, exactly where they had left them. Mounting their horses, they trotted through town, anxious and hopeful.

There was no sign of their friends.

"Maybe we should ask some of the townsfolk if they have seen them," Nell suggested.

"If they'll speak to us," Treyton muttered. "Don't forget, they were a wee bit angry before we fled."

As they rode through Paraan, they were shocked by the sight of flames leaping from the doorways of cottages and other buildings. Villagers scurried to put out the fires, while coils of black smoke traced a line into the sky.

"We have to help," Nell said, sliding to the ground.

Together, they helped the villagers carry water from the wells. Soon, the flames died out, leaving behind smoke and steam.

"Most of the people seemed happy to see us," Nell observed as she mounted her horse. "Contrary to their earlier behaviour."

Treyton nodded. "The Garshu's visit must have changed a few minds." His gaze swept over the smouldering buildings.

"I guess," Nell said.

A burial ceremony near the outskirts caught her eye.

Curious, she urged her horse forward, then dismounted and joined the mourners, careful not to interrupt.

A family of Elves stood over the body of a little girl. Lachlin and Bean stood nearby, while Garick spoke quietly to an Elvish woman who was wracked by grief.

Nell's heart ached for her. *Must be the girl's mother.*

She caught the end of the ceremony.

"...to sit beside Saros above," an ancient-looking Elf was saying. "Please protect Taraj and the family she has left behind. She will never be forgotten, so her kin will know her when they see her again. Taraj. Taraj. Taraj."

The mourners joined in, chanting the little girl's name, the tradition in Elvish funerary rituals.

Sobbing uncontrollably, the mother dropped to the girl's side. Solemn townsfolk drifted away, leaving her with the body. There would be no consoling her right now. An Elvish man tried to pry her from the gravesite so they could bury the body. The woman screamed in protest, fighting off the man with everything she had.

"Nell!"

Garick sprinted toward her, grabbed her and held her tight to his chest. Her muffled cry barely escaped.

"You are all right," he said. "Thank Saros."

As he set her free, she gasped for air. "I thought you wanted me alive."

Lachlin and Bean joined them.

"What happened here?" Treyton interrupted, surveying the sad scene.

"The Garshu—well, one in particular—killed her," Garick explained. "Out of spite. Because of me."

"Nay, that isn't true!" Lachlin cried. "He tried to save her, but the Garshulan slit her throat anyway. He wanted to kill someone. It just happened to be her." A look of heartbreak crossed her face.

Garick did not look so convinced of his innocence.

Treyton set a firm hand on his shoulder. "I'm sure it wasn't your fault."

Garick forced a small smile.

They set off in search of their three missing friends—

Liam, Karistaal and Peter. Passing the tavern, Bean disappeared inside.

"Bean!" Lachlin shouted.

She rolled her eyes at the young boy's impetuousness, and then trotted in after him.

A loud shriek followed.

"Quick!" Treyton shouted, rushing inside.

Once Nell entered the tavern, she discovered why Bean had dashed in. He had taken up arms next to Peter who was circling the room opposite a sprite of a man half his age—a loud-mouthed Dwarf.

"Weakling!" the Dwarf yelled.

"Imbecile!" Peter sneered.

"One-handed brute!"

They shouted insults back and forth, while drunken patrons pounded the bar and called for blood. None were really taking sides. They just wanted to watch a good show.

Nell searched the crowd for the others.

Karistaal waved. "Over here!"

They made their way to the corner where Karistaal was standing, her arms crossed and lips pursed in anger.

A glass of ale sailed over Nell's head and smashed into the wall behind her.

"Karistaal, what is going on?" she asked.

"We took cover in here when the Garshu arrived," the woman said. "And we'd have been found out because of that fatheaded Dwarf." She pointed at Peter's foe. "When he saw us hiding, he tried going after the Garshu to tell them we were here. Peter leapt on him, held him down until they left. Ever since, those two have been at each other's throats."

A mighty cheer exploded.

Even though the loss of a hand had Peter at a disadvantage, he had the Dwarf on his stomach. He held a paint-chipped stool over his head, about to clobber the little man. Just as the stool came down, the Dwarf rolled over and jumped to his feet.

Surprised, Peter swung with his good hand, hitting the

Dwarf square in the jaw. The Dwarf's head whipped back. Then he kicked Peter's legs out from underneath him. The old man hit the ground hard.

The crowd roared.

Fuelled by the chaos, the Dwarf leapt into the air, intending to land on Peter with his full, beefy weight. Peter struggled to his feet though, and caught the man in the air, swinging him around like a new bride.

Laughter trickled through the crowd.

The Dwarf's face turned pink with embarrassment. He scrambled from Peter's arms and grabbed a broken bottle from the ground. As he faced the old man, the audience grew quiet. The situation had just become far more serious.

"Should we help him?" Nell whispered.

Karistaal shook her head. "Let him play."

Peter glanced around for something to retaliate with, but to no avail. He shook his head when Bean offered a sword.

The Dwarf lunged at the old man, swiping the razor-sharp bottle at his face. Peter sidestepped to evade being cut, but stumbled onto a broomstick, which he swiftly lifted into the air with one foot. Passing it to his good hand, he lashed at the Dwarf and knocked him in the head.

The Dwarf stumbled, and then regained his balance. Losing his patience, he threw himself at Peter and knocked the old man onto his back. The Dwarf sat on top of him pushing the jagged bottle toward Peter's face. With both arms, Peter held off the Dwarfs' hands, grunting at the effort.

"Hold!" a voice commanded from the doorway.

Every head swivelled to see who dared to interrupt.

Nell gasped.

In the doorway, Liam held up his blood-spattered sword. Fatigue was etched on his grimy face and he had a massive crimson gash across his left leg.

Lachlin rushed over to her brother. "Liam, what—?"

Liam held up a hand. "They've sacked Cholart."

Gasps and cries filled the air, for many of the towns-folk had kin in their sister village.

"I rode ahead as soon as I heard the Garshu were coming," Liam explained. "It only took me a few moments to find a barn to hide in. Two Garshu rode into town. I've slain them both."

A fearful calm filled the room, many beyond speechless.

"Just when I had disposed of the bodies, the rest of the Garshu arrived. They burned down every building. And killed... *everyone.*" Tears filled Liam's exhausted eyes. "I tried to get back to fight, but I fell from my horse, too weak from my encounter with the two Garshu." He shook his head, perplexed. "I landed on my own sword blade. All I could do was watch the Garshu while they laughed as they cut off the fingers of Dwarven babies...one by one."

Outraged howls swept through the room.

Liam collapsed to the ground, unconscious, tears silently flowing from his eyes.

Chapter Eleven

Liam opened his eyes slowly, blinking as they adjusted to the bright rays of the sun. A tall shadow hovered over him, easing the piercing light. He made out an almost Human silhouette, but the ears were different. As the light dimmed, he saw long, flowing violet hair. It was pinned back. Then he made out intense grey eyes.

Anay looked down at him.

"Ah," she said. "You are awake."

A feeling of reassurance washed over Liam. Nothing creates more confidence after one is injured than knowing a Sarkian is tending.

He tried to sit up.

The Sarkian held up a hand. "Rest."

She quietly hummed an ancient lullaby, and he immediately drifted into a deep sleep.

Anay gathered her herbal rags and a pitcher of water, and then exited the cramped room. She walked into the open area of the bookshoppe, where Liam's friends anxiously awaited her return.

Lachlin was the first to greet her. "Will Liam be all right?" There was urgency in her tone.

Anay smiled. "He is well. He is resting."

The room breathed relief.

Lachlin left the room to sit with her brother.

When Liam had collapsed, Treyton had carried him to

the bookshoppe, where Nell pleaded for help. The Sarkians were more than happy to aid her, considering the news she had recently told them. Their medicinal skills were exceptional, outdone solely by Giant wisemen, whose enormous hands were far from clumsy since Saros had blessed them with a healing grace in their fingers.

Nell observed Anay. She was sterilizing the rags and emptying water from the pitcher.

"Thank you so much for helping my friend," Nell said.

Anay raised a hand and brought it close to Nell's face, so close that Nell could feel the warmth from it. Surprised at the woman's near stroke, she looked at her, thoroughly bewildered.

The Sarkian's eyes turned a cloudless opal—intense joy. "Nelhua, from the moment I met you, I sensed greatness from you. I believed it to be because you are Human, for greatness is said to be common with your kind. However, after meeting your friends, I have discovered it is not as common as one may think. You are *rare*, despite what they tell you. And they *will* tell you."

"They will?"

Anay's gaze deepened. "Do not heed their words. Follow your intuition, your soul's voice. It will never lead you astray, if you listen properly." The woman blinked.

Nell stumbled backward, released from Anay's gripping stare.

The woman lowered her hand and exited the room.

Everyone stared incredulously at Nell.

She breathed deeply, trying to shake a feeling of drowning intoxication. Not succeeding, she headed for the door and stepped out into the smoky air. She sat on the steps of the bookshoppe, trying to gather her senses.

The door opened behind her and she sensed someone.

"It was so odd, Garick," she murmured, staring at the ground. "I could see nothing when she was talking to me, but I sensed the most surreal calm. She relaxed me and frightened me all at once."

When she turned, Garick was leaning against the doorframe, eyes wide.

He let out a breath, and sat down beside her. "You know, your parents had remarkable intuition. They could sense so much. You seem to have inherited that noble gift, among many others."

She frowned. "I do not understand."

Garick gestured to the door. "You knew it was me, even though you did not turn around. You sensed my presence. What is even more amazing is you did not seem to notice yourself doing it. It was natural. You have done it before over the cycles, but I have never seen you do it as well as you did just now. You did not guess or suspect. You *knew*."

Nell did not know what to say. She could not deny that he was right, and she wondered if the Sarkian woman had anything to do with it. She pushed the thought aside, forcing her attention back to Liam.

"Has he woken?"

Garick shook his head, absent-mindedly searching the distance. His expression gave away what he felt. His regret over the murder of the Elf girl ate away at him.

"He will be asleep for a few hours, I think," he said.

Her eyes welled with tears. "Garick, what are we going to do?" She broke down, sobbing, releasing all the stress of the last few days.

"Oh, little one," Garick said gently, holding her.

"Everything is so…complicated."

She let go completely, spilling all of her heart's woes—Liam's kiss, her suspicions of Treyton's feelings, her idea to defeat the Garshu.

"Everyone is treating me like a child," she wept.

Garick rocked her, stroked her face and caressed her new red hair, its silkiness reminding him of how so many things had changed. Eventually, Nell fell into an oblivious state. Her breathing returned to normal and she gazed off into nothing. Warm air swept over them, and they held each other, while the scent of a burning town filled their nostrils.

"Let her be," Karistaal said, seizing Treyton's sleeve. "Garick is with her. And she needs naught but him right now."

Treyton protested, but relented when he saw her stern face. Annoyed, he yanked his arm away. "I wasn't going to help her, Kris. I was just going to get some fresh air."

"Oh yes, I'm certain you were," Karistaal said sarcastically.

"I was."

Karistaal rolled her eyes.

"I was!" he exploded.

Treyton stomped out of the room in a fit of fury and made for the front door. Karistaal stepped in to block his exit, her stoic eyes firm against his defiance. Exasperated, he headed for the back room where Liam was resting. There, the Sarkian woman, Anay, obstructed his attempt, not wanting him to disturb her patient.

He let out a frustrated roar, and then detoured around to the back door. Glaring over his shoulder at Karistaal, he rushed out, letting the door crash shut.

Karistaal looked over at Peter. He was reading in a corner chair. Bean stood beside him, staring out the window at the smoke rising from Cholart. Without a word, the boy strode out the back door behind Treyton.

Lachlin sat in a chair at Liam's bedside, her head resting on his evenly rising stomach as she held his hand in hers. Her eyes were closed tight and she sang a lullaby from their youth.

"*The Fae folk come to help you when hope is all but lost. High is the risk of action, but even higher is the cost.*"

She thought of when they were children, and recalled the nightmare that was real. Before long, she was in daze of painful memories.

When Liam suddenly grunted and tried to move his legs, she bolted upright, glad to be torn from such thoughts.

"You just sit there," she advised.

Liam settled back down and watched his sister reach for a rag. She began wiping the sweat from his face and neck.

"I don't remember coming here," he said. "Where are we, anyway?"

She attempted a smile. "At the Sarkian bookshoppe."

Liam smiled back, enjoying the peaceful moment with his sister. Without realizing, he closed his drowsy eyes and drifted into an uneasy sleep.

Lachlin watched her brother drift off and thought of her living nightmare—that horrible day on the beach. She had told Liam about making a life bond with the Mermaid, but she was certain he had not believed her. He had probably forgotten anyway.

She had not.

It haunted her every day. She grew more nervous as they traveled closer to the sea.

"Where is Lachlin?" Nell asked, returning to the bookshoppe. Garick trailed behind her.

"She's in with Liam," Karistaal answered, barely glancing up from the story she was pouring through. "I just checked on them. They are both sleeping."

She and Peter were sitting in a corner, taking advantage of all the books. Each had a small stack that they were looking through.

"We are heading home as soon as they wake," Nell announced. "All of our supplies and weapons are there. We have devised a plan that Treyton has already snuffed, but we are following through with it anyway."

Behind her, Garick reluctantly nodded.

"Well, do *we* not get our say?" Peter asked, rising from the chair. "Or does Treyton speak for us all?"

"Nay," a voice said.

Nell glanced over her shoulder at the back doorway.

Treyton was leaning against the frame.

"We are going to attack the Garshulas' nests," she

proclaimed. "I thought of doing a simultaneous attack, but there is too much risk involved. I have to research my new idea, but if I am right, we will be able to wipe out the Garshulas, which means—"

"No more breeding," Karistaal finished. "We would need only to kill the Garshulan. Brilliant!"

"And how do you expect to get into the nest?" Treyton inquired in a lazy drawl. "The nests are guarded by more Garshu than any of us have ever seen. Tales say they even have creatures protecting the Garshulas that only the Garshu have seen—creatures so horrible, it stops a man's heart to lay eyes on them."

Garick pursed his lips. "The Dukev."

Nell had heard of the creatures. Some said they were rodents the size of grown men, with huge paws. Other stories reported them to be twice the size of a man, with horns protruding from their foreheads and claws that could rip through bone.

Either way, she was more than ready to face them.

"I expect to encounter the Dukev," she said. "And I intend to destroy them and the Garshulas they are protecting. If you choose not to come, Treyton, so be it. Garick and I are leaving just as soon as we pick up some supplies. Then we will be heading home to gather what we need there. You are all welcome, for we intend to recruit anyone that will come with us. It will be a challenge."

Treyton strode toward Nell and whispered in her ear, his lips practically touching her face. "You realize that all our fates—our very lives—rest with this idea. Remember, if you fail, our race is doomed."

Nell looked him directly in the eye. "Then you had better make sure I do not fail."

Liam entered the room, leaning on a stick that Anay had given him. Lachlin stood beside him, eyebrows raised, a mix of shock and anger feuding in her expression. They shared the same thought.

Nell is standing far too close to Treyton.

Liam narrowed his eyes. "What's going on?"

Treyton and Nell stepped apart, as if just realizing they were facing each other so intimately.

"We are heading home," Nell blurted, eager to break the awkward silence. "We are going to gather supplies and rest. Then we are heading back here to recruit any who will join us before moving on to the Garshula nests. Are you with us?"

"Of course," Liam said. "We stay together."

His gaze fixed on Treyton, but his friend looked away.

"Right, then," Peter said. "Let us leave here."

Anay glided into the room and led Nell aside.

"Remember what I told you. Trust in yourself. You are the one person you can always count on."

Nell nodded.

Then Garick guided her out of the building.

"Wait!" Nell cried. "Where is Bean? Has anyone seen him?"

"He left with Treyton earlier," Peter said, helping Liam onto his horse. "But he didn't come back with him. Since he's not back by now, I'd say he's gone on one of his trips again."

"Trips?" Nell asked.

"Bean tends to run off every now and then," Karistaal explained. "He goes sometimes for weeks on end."

Nell was worried. "With all the Garshu roving, he will never be safe."

Karistaal gave a helpless shrug. "He never gets into any trouble. And even though we move around, he always seems to find us."

"Well, if he does this a lot," Garick said, settling on his horse, "then we should not dwell on it. Let us get moving."

Nell stared after him. He held his head and torso erect, his eyes hard and very far away. Her guardian's mood had become somewhat cool and fierce—ever since the funeral of the Elf girl. However, he seemed much more focused than ever.

She quickly mounted her horse, following a few paces after Garick. The others followed, including a very quiet and sad Lachlin, who kept her head lowered to hide the look of betrayal on her face. The vision of Treyton and Nell standing so close burned in her mind.

Riding beside her, Liam harboured his own misgivings. His face was stone and he was deep in thought. He was the only member of their group who was aware of how Lachlin was feeling. And *why*.

The riders exchanged looks with the townsfolk as they passed through the village. Some faces bore sheer hatred, while others wore expressions of hopeful reliance.

Nell caught up with Garick. "Do you think Bean is okay? He is so young, after all."

"I'm sure he is fine."

Nell was taken aback. Garick sounded irritated. He had never used that tone before.

She slowed her horse and joined Treyton. He gave her an uncertain look, then glanced away.

Frustrated, she fell back further.

"Lachlin," she said, relieved. "Ride with me."

But she found no reciprocation. Instead, Lachlin's cold, teary eyes bore into hers, until Nell finally tore her gaze away. She was left eating Lachlin's dust.

Karistaal reigned in alongside her, smiling warmly. When Peter came up on Nell's other side, she began to feel better.

"Would you like to hear a story?" he asked.

She nodded. "I would."

The older Human searched his memory for a moment. Then he took a deep breath. *"Across the seas, there is a land, across the waves, across the sand; it is cursed, this land of woe, no God to love—no one would go."*

Nell's smile grew as the familiar story was laid before her. For a brief moment, Peter's voice whisked her off to faraway lands, helping her to forget all about icy stares, missing friends and the vicious Garshu.

Chapter Twelve

As they neared the farm, Garick's mind was made up. After tending to the horses, he marched into the cottage and went straight to his room. Once inside, he furiously began sorting through his clothes.

Nell passed by his doorway.

"What are you doing?" she asked, frowning as Garick thrust his belongings into a sack.

He took her hands and led her to the bed.

"Nell, I need to take care of something before we go to the caves. It is very important to me. Now that these people are here, I think I can leave you in safe hands."

"Leave me?"

He sighed, and then eyed the closet. "This is not easy for me. When I took you in, I was very young. I believed the best way to keep you safe was to let everyone believe you were...dead. That is why there have been no search parties sent after you. And why everyone was so surprised to learn who your parents were."

"People think I died?" she asked in disbelief.

He nodded. "No one believed you survived the Garshu attack. And in order to keep your survival a secret, I had to let people believe I had died as well." His eyes were an ocean of sorrow about to overflow. "My family never knew what happened to me, for I could not risk their safety by letting them know I had survived too.

I have not seen them in thirteen cycles."

Nell felt sick at seeing the strongest person she knew in utter turmoil. Guilt swept over her like an icy wind. She could not believe this had not occurred to her before. *Of course Garick had a family.*

Sensing her shame, Garick shook his head. "Nell, I do not regret one second of the time we have spent together. Nor do I regret the choice I made all those cycles ago. I would not trade any of it for all the wealth of Cantro." He cupped her chin. "I did it because you are a daughter of Saros. But also because I love you for who you are inside, Nelhua Sahnatru."

He reached for her and hugged her tightly. When they finally broke apart, they sat in silence for a long moment.

"I remember you cried that day," he said in a sad voice. "You cried, screamed, and batted at me, but I had to do it. I had to make you look Elvish. The cutting of your hair was the worst. You would not sit still and I was terrified I would cut you. I had to use a small dagger. Later, when I was shaving your head, it was easier. You were so exhausted from fighting me; you just sat back and let me finish. I had to secretly steal clothes from my little sister. Then I burned the ones you were wearing. I did keep this for you though."

He pulled a small bracelet of twine from the pocket of his tunic. With awkward movements, he fastened it around her wrist and kissed her cheek.

"You were wearing it that day, Nell. The day your parents were killed. Afterward, I had to steal currency for us to live on and to build this cottage. It was hard for a long time, because you were so young. I had to go off and earn us currency, and still keep an eye on you. It was cycles before I was able to function properly and raise you as a normal child. I am just glad you do not remember. There were so many...hard times." He squeezed his eyes shut, trying to force away the memories.

Nell placed a hand on his shoulder. "Garick, thank you. You have sacrificed so much for me. I owe you my life."

"Well, I do love you, little one."

With a smile, he walked to the closet and locked it. Then he took Nell's hand and placed the key in it.

"I will reach my family's home in less than four days," he said. "You will not open this door before seven days have passed. That will give you enough time to sort through what you will find. I will be back soon after."

He studied her face for a long moment. "Do not even think of using this key before the seventh day."

He kissed her forehead, and then took one last look around the room. Grabbing the sack, he headed for the kitchen, with a stunned Nell trailing after him. He grabbed two loaves and a large chunk of meat. Then he filled his flask with water.

With a quick nod, Garick vanished out the door.

"What do you mean seven days?" Liam demanded. "We don't have that kind of time."

Nell had gathered them at the dining table.

"Liam, that is the timeline," she said. "Garick will not be back before then, Bean has not yet returned, and you still need time to mend. Do not forget, the townsfolk are counting on us to be in Paraan in a fortnight. Seven days will give us the opportunity to contact several towns and enlist any who will join us. Since Treyton knows the lands to the south, I will go to the north. We must prepare ourselves for the journey."

"Nay," Liam argued. "It's too dangerous. And you're not ready."

Her green eyes fired darts. "When *will* I be ready in your eyes? Maybe when we are all dead? Or perhaps many cycles from now when I am an old woman."

"Aye, you'll have more sense then, I think," he muttered. "*I'll* go north. Yes, Treyton should go south. He's been there before."

Defiance was etched on Nell's face.

"Fine," she agreed through gritted teeth. "Liam heads to Santz and up to Vynoor. We should stay away from

Lendor right now. It runs too close to where the Garshu are raiding. Treyton, you go through Sorcha Forest to Bryonn and Fairsome. I will head west to Pandrag, then over to Ronif. Kris and Peter will stay here with Lach—"

"I don't think so, my dear," Peter interjected. "Liam is still mending, so I will accompany him north. Lachlin will accompany you west, for Kris is more than capable of preparing without us. It's best if we go in pairs anyway." He winked at Treyton. "Except for you, boy. You're too impossible to pair up with."

"Well, at least I am not the only one who thinks so," Nell said coldly.

Lachlin cleared her throat. "Maybe I should go with Liam. Or with Treyton. I don't like the villages to the west." She glanced at Nell with a look of distaste. "They are full of dimwitted traitors."

"I think Nell needs your company," Peter insisted. "You should go, Lach."

"If she does not want to come with me," Nell said quietly, "let her aid someone else."

Peter shook his head. "No. This is our plan. Now we pack. The days will pass quicker than any of us are ready for."

Upon entering Pandrag, Nell was nervous. Even her horse seemed a bit skittish. Nell had only been to tiny Paraan a few times in her life, and here she was marching into a major city. She was surprised to discover that it was not much different from Paraan. There was just a lot more of everything, and it was far bigger.

She also found Pandrag much more desolate.

The gates were no longer guarded, as they once were by the Controlice. They were tied open. Judging from their state, they had not been used in many a cycle. It was obvious the Garshu had already been there. Buildings were black from ash and smoke, and practically every window had been blown out by an explosion. Families lived behind rags that hung from windowsills and their waste littered the streets, while the cries of the sick filled Nell's ears.

She leaned over to Lachlin. "Are all the large cities like this?"

Lachlin nodded. "They are in recent cycles. Treyton wasn't teasing when he said the Garshu were terrorizing others. It's just gotten worse here, that's all. They keep the people poor."

Nell's grandiose visions of golden cities and a world quite unlike her own were quickly fading away. She had never seen such suffering.

Nevertheless, the day's findings were fruitful, considering the circumstances. Two young Human women coming into the city to raise hopes of a rebellion against Garshu raiders were an unusual sight. Half the citizens of Pandrag were too shocked at seeing the women to focus on what they were saying. Others simply laughed at them, thinking that an attack on the Garshu was a crazy idea.

"Like bees, they will swarm us," one Dwarf woman muttered. "And their weapons don't sting—they burn,"

"We will outnumber them if we just stand up and fight," Nell urged. "We have a plan. Bring security to your children and grandchildren. Do you want them to suffer as you all have? To live in fear and be constantly hunted? Join with us and set them free."

Many heads nodded, inspired by her piety to the cause.

Word about the rebellion spread quickly throughout the city. Before long, the women had shaken hands with hundreds of townsfolk who swore their loyalty. However, Lachlin and Nell could not leave without many also cursing their presence. They left the borders wearing streaks of rotten food, the outcries of Pandragians ringing garishly in their ears.

The blackness of the night convinced the women to camp along the outer wall of Pandrag. Keeping the fire low, they warmed the stew Karistaal had sent with them. They ate in silence.

Nell peeked at Lachlin, but the woman ignored her and thoughtfully stared west.

"I think it went well today," Nell said.

Lachlin nodded, her mouth full and her mind faraway.

"Many will come, I think," Nell added. "More than I expected. Pandrag is quite the city. I have never been in one so big before. Garick never took me anywhere except Paraan. I…" She trailed off as Lachlin stared at her, a look of cynical confusion on her face.

"What?" Nell asked. "Why are you looking at me like that?"

Lachlin looked away, west of course, then glanced back at Nell. "I have been horrible to you. Yet here you sit, gabbing away to me as though I were your closest friend. No one talks to me like that."

"No one talks to me at all," Nell said. "At least you have grown up with a family around you. As much as I love Garick, it is nice to talk to another female."

"Nell, there is something you should know." Lachlin looked down at her covered palms. "I wear these gloves for a reason. Saros has blessed me with an unusual gift of vision. Although at times it seems a curse."

"I know about your gift," Nell said, reaching into the sack and pulling out an apple. "I grew up with not much to do but read. Once I found out I was Human, I read many books on our race and our gifts. I am learned in many things, one of them being the symptoms of Revelation-Foresight." She leaned in. "You do not hide your gift very well." She smiled.

Lachlin raised an eyebrow, but smiled too. She wanted so much to dislike Nell, but could not.

"You seem wise for your age," she said. "But I guess that's expected, being raised by an Elf. Elves are much more focused in their studies, as well as in most things."

"Aye," Nell agreed.

The women sat quietly, braided together by their thoughts.

Finally, Nell spoke. *"The two stars shone strong, a friendship began; like a Goddess song, Janell and*

Moran."

Lachlin's eyes widened at hearing the familiar verse about a warrior woman and her sister. The poem told about their estrangement and reunion.

She looked at Nell in surprise.

Nell returned her gaze with a thoughtful grin.

Chapter Thirteen

Liam and Peter stood on the outskirts of Santz. They were hiding behind some palm-leafed bushes, their horses concealed not far behind them in a copse of trees. The men remained quite stealthy, and rightly so, for they were watching the Garshu exit the village. Earlier, they had witnessed the creatures taking supplies without payment, and then tormenting local farmers.

The two men finally crept into the town, wrapped in heavy hooded cloaks to disguise themselves.

"We need to find out if all the Garshu are gone," Peter stated. "Before we do anything."

Liam nodded, his eyes inspecting their surroundings.

They agreed to split up, get a feel for the village first to see how many loyalists there would be. They each withdrew an hourglass from their pockets and arranged to meet in the same spot after one full turning. Shaking hands robustly, Liam and Peter separated and took to their missions.

Peter entered a tavern, the title above the door missing several letters, dubbing the inn, *Th Coy Drag n.*

Once inside, the raucous laughter and yelling of drunken husbands and feisty concubines deafened him. Luckily, there were no Garshu to be seen.

He found a stool near the end of the grimy, ale-soaked bar, and signalled the seedy Dwarf to bring him the house special. The Dwarf splashed the ale down in front of him, peering into the hood. Peter lowered his head and dropped a coin onto the bar. The barkeep snarled and picked up the currency, and Peter let out a sigh of relief as the barkeep walked back to his sink.

"What brings you to Santz, stranger?"

Peter tilted his head at the Elf standing beside him. The man was old and wore a ragged tunic and pants. His clothing was caked in dried mud, as was the Elf himself.

"My home has been destroyed by Garshu," Peter said. "I am seeking new quarters. Tell me, friend, do the Garshu terrorize you as well?"

The Elf seemed surprised, and Peter was afraid he had been too forward. Then the Elf slumped onto the stool beside him and set his drink upon the bar.

"The Garshu are always here now," the Elf whispered. "They have taken an interest in our metal trade. This city puts out the best armour and weapons in all of Cantro. If no one disagrees with them, no one dies. If it is the Garshu you fear, friend, then I would not seek refuge here."

He stood, took the last swig of his ale and slammed the empty glass down.

Liam found it difficult to discover an alleyway or road free of Garshu. Streets were lined with deteriorating buildings and every few heartbeats a door or window revealed a Garshulan. They swarmed the city, their hissing voices a constant din in the air, like a voluminous cloud that never ascended. Every tavern he peeked into had Garshu lining the bar or ravaging the concubines.

He finally found an inn with an empty foyer, and he entered cautiously. A young Elf woman at the greeting table looked up, her eyes fearful. When she saw the cloaked figure, she seemed to ease.

"Are you looking for shelter, visitor? We have nice

warm rooms with solid beds. Cook makes a hearty stew, and I…"

Liam held up a hand, while watching the girl from the darkness of his hood. "I'm looking for information. Why are the Garshu in such number here?"

The young woman's face drained of colour and she nervously played with a silver bracelet on her wrist. Glancing around the room, she leaned forward. "They are everywhere now. Rumour has it they are amassing against a group of foreigners. We have metal smiths that the Garshu have taken an interest in. They forge day and night."

Her eyes were red from long nights of crying. "I have not seen my father or brothers for nearly a cycle now. They are always working at the pits, creating weapons for the Garshu. I cannot see them from the entrance, and if I go in, the Garshu will make me work too. We have no choice."

"Yes, you do," Liam said firmly. "I'm no foreigner." He drew back his hood and the girl gasped. "And if you listen, I'll tell you about your choice."

He told her of the rebellion. The fiery light in the woman's eyes told Liam there would be many in Santz willing to fight.

An hour after their separation, Liam and Peter met back at their horses.

"Perhaps we should look in on these pits?" Peter said. "There may be something going on that we need to know about."

Despite the throbbing in his leg, Liam agreed. "These people must be terrified living among the Garshu."

They quickly mounted and followed the cloud of smoke that plumed above the southern border of the city. When they crested a slight hill, they spotted the gaping pits and their eyes widened in horror. Past huge iron gates, the metal smith's shop had been partially demolished and the area turned into a mass work camp.

Elves and Dwarves of all ages were led by ropes around their necks. Those that lagged were cut free and thrown into the rocky chasms that surrounded the slaves. Enormous fires were lit in the shallow holes and the filthy workers sweat as they forged, a whip at their back.

"Saros help us," Peter murmured.

Leaving their horses, they crept closer and crouched behind a boulder at the hill's base. When they were in position, they peeked around the rock.

Garshu flooded the camp, strange swords in their hands as they shouted orders.

"They're speaking another language!" Peter hissed, stunned.

The Garshu's voices did not hiss as much, but the words sounded slippery and foreign. They spoke to each other in the strange tongue, while whipping the citizens who worked and stabbing the ones who fell behind.

"I don't think we should be here," Liam whispered. "Let's leave for Vynoor."

With one last look at the pit, they moved discreetly up the hill.

"Something is very wrong."

As he approached his family's cottage, Garick slowed his horse to a plodding walk and scanned the ground in horror. He was prepared for anger, sadness, even banishment—but that was all. He did not expect this.

The cottage was only a shadow of its former loveliness. In what was once a lush, beautiful garden, patches of dead roots were scattered and forgotten, while the pathway to the cottage was lined with overgrown weeds. Pieces of shattered wood littered the perimeter, blown off by some force. Windows were naked of their glass and the outer walls were abundant with black scorch marks.

Garick's stomach tightened as he dismounted. He sprinted to the front door. It was encased in cobwebs and slightly ajar. Using both hands, he fought to open the stiff door, its stale creaking echoing throughout the cottage.

He knew it was deserted. But he called out anyway. "Hello?"

The only reply was the empty daylight that streamed in through the glassless windows.

He entered the dining hall. An overturned oak dining table and its chairs littered the room. He passed the huge table and refused to imagine what could have upset it. He knelt down next to it and ran his hands down the side, his fingers stopping on an indentation in the wood.

A memory flickered in his mind.

He had been barely seventeen when he had carved his initials into the lumber. Something was different about it now. Confused, he looked down and saw that his mark had been scratched out. Three swift slices through it revealed what he had feared.

"They evicted me from their minds and hearts."

Standing, he fought back emotional tears. He turned on the spot and saw that raids and rats had cleaned out the cupboards. Empty sacs that once held flour and seeds were strewn carelessly on the floor.

"No more tears." he chastised.

He moved further into the cottage. The bedrooms were in the same state, strewn with random belongings and what was left after the raids. In fact, all the rooms— once decorated in ornaments and family heirlooms— were nearly bare.

"They left hastily," he said. "And without warning."

Rounding a hall corner, he lurched to a stop.

A stain before his feet blocked his way. A burgundy blotch had soaked into the solid wood floors of the vast sitting area. The stain appeared to have been there for many cycles.

Then Garick saw something even more horrifying.

Lifeless bodies lay on the floor near the far wall.

"No!" he shrieked, running to them.

What was left of his father was hunched at the foot of a chair, the side of his face on the floor. He was crouched as though he had been sitting when death took him, as if he had been knocked off the chair and then stiffened with time. Garick's mother was curled up on the floor in the corner opposite his father, her dull dead eyes watching the man she loved. Both had been stripped of their clothing, and since Elves do not deteriorate with death and were buried only for spiritual purposes, the scene before Garick was particularly heinous.

He rushed outside, his mind boiling with grief and hopelessness. Raising his arms to Saros, he bellowed in absolute rage, a throaty and powerful roar.

"*Death to all Garshu!*"

He fell to his knees, freed from his fury. Exhausted and worn with anguish, he lay in the dead grass and closed his eyes.

After concealing his horse in the hills, Treyton entered the Bryonn city limits on foot and quickly slid behind a tree.

Garshu were everywhere. They hassled merchants and bothered townsfolk. Some just mulled around—eyes searching all about for their next victims.

Treyton slid from his hiding place and walked briskly down an alley. The echoes of his weathered boots ricocheted off the grey brick as he tugged his hood forward as far as it would go.

He paused.

The hissing of Garshu was all around. Then he saw their shadows dancing on the brick in front of him.

They were coming closer.

Before they could spot him, he seized the nearest door handle and it jangled open. His senses exploded as he slipped inside and quickly closed the door behind him.

When he turned, his eyes widened with surprise.

The room was enveloped in several different fragrances. Herbs burned strong and true, and there were plates of smoking pebbles that he had never seen before. Jewellery and trinkets garnished the walls, causing them to glitter with fresh ambiance.

Admiring the strange and alluring items, he began to

set his hood back when he heard a scuffling. He jerked the hood forward and his hand went inside his cloak to his sword. Faint laughter, like tiny bells, came from behind.

He turned.

Through an archway, a tiny woman emerged, carrying a gold serving tray. She wore a strange-looking dress and her braided silver hair dragged on the floor. Her features were Elvish and very attractive, but Treyton had never seen an Elf so short.

She shuffled past him, setting the tray down on a table between two elegant chairs. She glanced at Treyton and giggled again. Struggling, she finally managed to get up on one of the chairs. She poured a cup of tea, gingerly sipped it, and then set it in her lap.

"Are ye goin' to stare at me all day, Treyton? Or will you drink some tea 'fore it cools?"

At this, he snapped out of his trance.

The woman poured some tea and handed him the cup.

"I've never seen an Elf with hair before," he said, sitting across from her. "Who are you and how do you know my name?"

"I know much, Human. More than ye would like me to, I imagine."

Treyton stared in astonishment at the woman. "Who are you?" He tossed his hood back.

"Citizens here call me De'Lenrais." She shrugged. "My companions just call me Deni. I look strange to ye because I am of Elvish and Human ancestry. With yer upbringing, you've never seen one like me before. That is why ye thought I was Elf-kind, until you saw my hair and height." She patted the silver braid at her side.

"I've never seen hair so light on someone so young," Treyton noted.

Deni's eyes sparkled. "I'm older than ye think. My lotions keep my appearance young, and the citizens pay dearly fer them and my other ointments."

He smirked. "Oh, you're a Withican. Witch-kind."

Deni waved her hand dismissingly. "I just make things and sell them. I'm a merchant." She winked. "However, I also see things and can tell of them."

Treyton frowned.

"Fear not, Human," the woman continued. "I won't reveal yer presence. My own presence here is practically unknown—only protected by my Elf bloodlines. My door was unlocked because I knew ye would be entering it."

Deni gestured to the teapot. "I even made us tea. Saros knows we need ye and yer friends to fulfill yer destinies."

His eyes grew wide. "How do you know these things?"

Deni smirked, motioning for his hands.

Cautiously, he set them on the table, palms up, and the woman placed her forefingers on his wrists. Her eyes flickered, but remained open. Treyton watched, frozen, as they clouded over and changed hues. Blues, greens, violets, browns.

Suddenly, Deni's eyes cleared. She removed her hands.

Taking a deep breath, she smiled. "Ye love her. That is good. It will bring about great sadness for some, but it's for the best."

Treyton frowned in confusion.

"Oh, and you must let him go after the tragedy," Deni said, sliding off the chair and moving away. "He will return in time."

Treyton jumped to his feet, confused. "What are you talking about? Love whom? What tragedy? What did you just do?"

Deni turned. "I suffered yer lifelines, yer blood. I already knew yer past, and now I know yer future, if you make the right choices."

Giggling like a child, she shuffled out of the room.

Treyton was left alone, perplexed.

Chapter Fourteen

Nell jerked on the reins and stopped her horse dead in its tracks. She and Lachlin were halfway to Ronif, but a sudden consuming chill made her feel as though her veins were pumping ice rather than blood. She closed her eyes, trying to focus on the sensation and where it had originated.

Loss...pain...

"Garick!"

Nell kicked her horse into a full gallop.

Lachlin was baffled. Although she did not understand the urgency, she followed Nell.

"What's wrong?" she shouted.

Nell dismissed all of her attempts to find out.

They rode the rest of the day, stopping briefly and then continued to ride all night. They reached the cottage in the early morn.

Nell jumped off her horse and ran inside, barely acknowledging Karistaal. She ran straight into Garick's room and pulled out the key from around her neck.

Karistaal and Lachlin scurried after her.

"Nell, what's wrong?" Karistaal asked. "How was the journey? You're back early." She dried her hands on some linen and glanced at Lachlin, signalling her confusion.

Lachlin shrugged, clearly irritated. "We rode non-stop."

Ignoring them, Nell stood at the door of the closet, the tip of the key scarcely brushing the lock. Her hands shook when Garick's warning rang in her ears.

"Do not even think of using this key before the seventh day."

Recalling the strange feeling she had had yesterday, she shoved the key into the lock. It clicked softly. As she swung the closet door open, a waft of lavender blew over her face. She reached for one of the candles that Garick kept on the shelf next to the closet and struck a match.

Inside, papers were stacked high on various shelves, and ornaments and figurines were displayed prominently. What caught her eye most, however, was the drape at the back of the closet. It was pulled back, revealing a descending stairway formed of dirt and mud, hardened and shaped through the cycles.

Karistaal and Lachlin, silent in their curiosity, squeezed in behind her as she stepped inside. They followed as Nell gingerly moved down the steps, her mouth agape at the markings and designs that adorned the walls. Strangely beautiful, the symbols were uniform, so she knew they spelled or intended a form. Though from all her studies, they still seemed foreign to her. The women trailing behind her held the same disbelieving stare. When they reached the bottom of the steps, they saw a massive room. It had been underneath the cottage all along.

In the darkness, Nell could make out some wooden crates. On top of one was a candle. She lit it. Another candle was visible on her left and she held a flame to it as well. She lit candle after candle, until she found herself back at the base of the stairway.

Karistaal let out a low whistle.

The room was aglow, its earthen walls draped in fabric and garnished with an abundance of swords that shone and glimmered like serpentine gems.

Nell could not even begin to count them.

"This must be where Garick hid those swords from me," she said, bemused.

Crates, barrels and sacks were stockpiled at the far end, overflowing with clothing and a variety of weapons. The far right corner held a burlap sack and the largest crate.

Neither was opened.

Nell made a beeline for them and used a sword to pry off the crate's lid. Exotic foods occupied the box, their strange scents penetrating her nostrils. She glanced at the sack. It was big enough to hold a small child. She untied the rope that bound it and currency of every type jingled to the floor. Meethaars, sanaars and more dyjaars than Nell had ever dreamt of.

Lachlin let out a strangled cough, while Karistaal gasped and dropped the clothing in her hands.

Then all three crowded around the sack, each of them reaching in, allowing the coins to trickle like sand through their fingers.

Nell gestured to a crate in the other corner.

"What is over there?"

"Documents," Lachlin said. "Lots of them, all marked with strange letters. It's a language I've never seen before."

They made their way to the crate and Karistaal picked up one of the papers. Her eyes softened at what she saw.

"This is the language of Saros. It is ancient Achocra, the tongue of Shirell." Her eyes faded, lost in a far away memory. "This is the language Human families recorded their histories in. It was believed the Garshu had destroyed all the records in their burnings."

She sifted through the pile. "Garick has been busy, Nell. It looks like he has found many different lineage records."

"He has been busy indeed," Nell murmured.

The women stood in the dank room, each with difficulty fathoming their discovery.

Lachlin finally broke the silence.

"How long have you known about this place, Nell?"

"Garick has kept his closet secret," Nell replied. "I knew he had several things he wished to keep hidden from me, but I had no idea about *this*."

She spread her arms out, although the gesture could not symbolize the magnitude of the findings.

"When he left four days ago, he left me the key to the closet. He said not to open it until seven days had passed. But as we drew near Ronif, I sensed great pain."

"Whose pain?" Karistaal demanded.

Nell sighed. "Garick is in overwhelming anguish. He will be back much sooner, and I knew I needed to come home and open the closet. I-I just sensed a sudden urgency. I cannot explain."

Karistaal placed a comforting arm around Nell's shoulders. "It is hard to adjust to new sensations. I imagine with parents like yours, your intuition is unusually strong."

She gestured to Lachlin. "Lachlin's visions are quite jarring for her. They are different from normal visions. The rest of us just witness, but she's forced to experience." She moved between Nell and Lachlin, hugging them close. "My talented, wearied girls."

Footsteps stomped overhead.

"Hello?" Peter called. "Where are you, my love?"

The women looked at each other and smirked.

Karistaal smirked. "Peter! Come here, won't you?"

The women moved to the base of the stairs.

Peter was first to enter the secret room, his confusion prominent on his brow. Liam followed.

Lachlin grasped him immediately. "How is your leg?"

"I'm fine," he murmured.

"What is this?" Peter breathed, eyeing the swords and various sacks.

"Aye, what?" Liam said, equally entranced.

"We have just discovered this," Karistaal explained. "It seems Garick has been a busy Elf. He has been gathering these things for many a cycle, I'd guess."

Lachlin sorted through a sack of clothes, while Nell remained at the base of the stairs and watched as Karistaal showed the documents to Peter. Nell remembered the pain she sensed the day before.

When will Garick return?

"Aye," she heard Peter say.

He and Karistaal studied her.

Nell frowned. "What?"

"This is all for you," Peter said. "Garick has gathered and saved all of this for you. He either knew that you would fight the Garshu and need certain things, or he believed you to be the last Human and he preserved ways of life for you. Whichever it is, that Elf has gone to incredible lengths for you, little one."

Humbled by Peter's words, she fled upstairs.

Treyton's visit to Fairsome did not go as pleasantly as he had hoped. Once he snuck past the Garshu at the gates, he stepped foot into the city and a panicky old Dwarf woman had somehow identified him.

"Human!" she bellowed across the skies.

He was forced to flee further into the city, since the Garshu at the gates were now looking for the cause of the woman's cry. He streaked through the city, finding refuge at the first merchant stand he could find. He leapt behind it, just as the Garshu rushed past him, their weapons unsheathed.

Nearby, a garishly thin Elvish farmer cowered under his cart. The Elf's eyes widened at seeing him, flickering in alarm.

Treyton brought his finger to his lips. *"Shh!"*

The Elf grinned, then crawled from beneath his cart. "Human!"

Treyton hissed his annoyance and set off again, this time down an alleyway that led to an enormous square filled with townsfolk. He skidded to a halt and ducked into an entrance. When he poked his head from the doorway, he gasped at the horrifying sight that greeted him.

The Dwarf woman was being hung.

"Let thisss be a lessson to you all," a Garshulan leader said. "Do not attempt to ssstrike fffear into the heartsss of

Garshu with liesss of Humansss running around our city."

He kicked out the stool that the woman teetered on.

She dropped.

The sound of her neck snapping ricocheted off the brick buildings in the square.

No one said a word.

Then Treyton heard a whimpering cry to his left.

The Elvish man was dragged into the square.

"I know I saw one!" the man cried. "Please, sir, I have a family to look after. I only told you because I thought you might show us mercy if you were given a Human."

The Garshulan leader loosened the noose around the dead Dwarf's neck and her lifeless body crumpled into the dirt. He kicked her corpse aside, then looked at the Garshulan escorting the Elf.

"He wants us to show mercy."

The Garshu roared with gurgling laughter.

"Mercy?" The Garshulan leader sneered at the Elf. "Had there been a Human here, we would have killed it. And then you."

He pushed the Elf's head into the loop, tightening it. The other Garshulan tugged on the rope until the Elf had no choice but to climb onto the stool.

The Elf whimpered, then his terrified gaze fell upon Treyton, pleading silently and more convincingly than any words could.

"I can't believe I'm considering this," Treyton muttered.

He bent down in the doorway and pulled a dagger from his boot.

"No more nonsssenssse," the Garshulan said. "Unlesss the whole lot of you want to be ssstretched." He lifted his foot to kick out the stool.

The dagger whizzed through the air, severing the rope.

The scrawny Elf dropped to the dirt, the dagger firmly planted into the wood of the gallows where he had hung mere seconds earlier.

The Garshulan roared in anger, searching the square for the owner of the dagger. He found only fleeing citizens who did not want to incur his wrath.

The Elf glimpsed at the doorway.

It was empty.

He bolted from the square and headed straight for his cart. Shoving all the merchandise and fruit inside, he flipped up the sides and secured them. Then he lifted the handles from the ground and jogged out of the city gates, red-faced from the weight of the cart. The severed noose still hung limply from his neck. Leaving Fairsome, he rushed down the path toward Sorcha Forest.

Ahead, a shadow ducked into the trees.

The Elf quickened his pace.

Nell's dreams were feverish and fiery. She dreamt the same one she always did, of metal boots and a creature stinking of rancid meat, and she could never awake fast enough.

Bolting upright, she found her bearings and scooted out of bed. Garick would be home soon, and she wanted to be sure that everything was ready for his arrival.

She dressed and headed for Garick's closet.

When she entered, she saw light flickering at the bottom of the stairway.

The others were already hard at work. Lachlin stood in the corner, organizing the clothes, while Liam and Peter sat cross-legged in the middle of the floor and sorted the currency that had been tossed at random into the sacks. Karistaal had already unpacked the food. Some of it had spoiled, but most of it was non-perishable.

"Ah, you're awake," Karistaal greeted her. "Perhaps you can sort through the papers over there."

"What shall we do with all this food?" Nell asked.

"I'll take it upstairs for Garick," Karistaal said. "It's mostly Elvish food and the scents are rather…offensive."

Nell wrinkled her nose and gave a brief nod.

She now understood why her guardian had hidden the food. She would not have liked it, and it would have been another strike against convincing her that she was an Elf.

As she passed through the room, she noticed several Elvish recipe books.

"I think I will prepare a special dish for Garick's return," she said.

Then she set to her appointed task, sorting through the paperwork that Garick had piled up over the cycles.

Nell picked up a sheet of paper with odd symbols on it.

"I have no idea what that says," Peter said, moving near.

"I do," she said in a dazed voice. "Garick always said I had a natural talent for language."

Astonished eyes met hers.

"I can translate most of the languages here." She waved a hand over the yellowed pages in front of her. "Including ancient Achocra. It is one of the languages I learned in my studies. But I never realized its importance."

She looked at Karistaal. "Until now."

"Nell," Peter said. "You realize no one can read the ancient tongue anymore. All who could...have perished."

She continued to organize the papers, but Peter's words echoed in her heart, making her feel more alone than she ever had before.

For Garick, the ride home was long. A sense of hopelessness engulfed him the moment he left his family home. The memory of his departure hung from him like heavy regret.

He had gone through the cottage to see if there were any belongings worth salvaging. Of course, he found nothing and was drawn back to the engraving on the table. By the time he had given his parents a proper burial and looked over the cottage once again, the day was late.

Still, he stared at the table.

His rage finally overcame him and he stormed outside

to the woodshed. An old rusty axe in hand, he burst into the cottage.

He roared, slicing into the weathered wood with furious accuracy. He chopped and screamed until his arms and head felt as though they might fall apart.

Then he finally stopped.

Drenched in sweat and tears, Garick reached into the wreckage of splintered wood and picked up a small square of lumber. He turned it over. The tainted initials brought more tears, and he fell to his knees once again.

"I will seek justice. I swear!"

Gaining his composure, he staggered to his feet and tore a piece of fabric from his shirt. He wrapped the block of wood in it and placed it in his pocket. He reached into his other pocket and pulled out some matches, striking one against the wall. He held it out in front of him, mouthed an Elvish prayer of cleanliness into the flame, and then dropped the match.

It fell between the piles of timber and began to smoke.

On his way out the door, Garick spat on what his childhood home had become because of the Garshu.

"Time to head back," he muttered.

On his journey home, his hand drifted to his pocket, more than once. Each time he touched the fabric-wrapped wood, his anger grew a little more. He dwelled on the times he could have visited, had Nell never come into his life. Then he remembered how much he loved her. He could never have let harm come to her. All of this—his leaving, his staying away, his family's death—was because of the Garshu.

Something happened to him the instant he came to that realization. A tranquil enlightenment devoured him and he would have been at peace were it not for the blistering ball of vengeance quietly docking in his gut. He knew he had been changed, and from that moment on, no Garshulan would escape his arrows.

He kicked his horse into a canter.

"He approaches!" Karistaal hollered from the garden.

Nell bustled around in the kitchen, nervousness thwarting her movements. She knew that something had happened to Garick, that he would arrive early, and now she was anxious to see him and make sure he was all right.

All afternoon, she had prepared a meal for him. The Elvish food clashed with her senses as she laid out the final pieces of the meal on a plate for her guardian, and soon she heard Garick's horse whinny outside. Then she heard his voice as he paid a curt greeting to Karistaal.

Garick entered the kitchen and laid eyes on her grinning face. His gaze went from her to the plate of food and back to her. Puzzled, he picked up the dish, examining the food. Suddenly, he threw the plate against the wall, smashing it and scattering food everywhere.

He stepped toward her, one arm raised. "You have opened the closet! I told you…seven days!"

Nell cowered and her eyes wide with fear.

Staggering, Garick lowered his arm. He took a breath to calm himself, then realized he was already composed, his pulse slow.

"I am sorry, Nell," he said with a groan. "I…I did not mean to scare you. I would not harm you."

A shadow passed from his face. He stroked her cheek and felt shame as she flinched at his touch.

"I sensed your anguish," her voice quivered. "You told me to open the closet before you came home, but I knew you would arrive early. I *sensed* it!"

Garick hugged her to his chest and looked over her head at the others. Liam, Lachlin, Karistaal and Peter stared at him sadly.

Chapter Fifteen

Treyton's journey back to the farm through Sorcha Forest was uneventful, right up until his second morning. He'd had a suspicion he was being followed and took utmost care at remaining stealthy, often veering his horse off the path and weaving through the trees. He made camp the night before deep into the bushes.

That morning, he discovered the Elf hidden within a small cover of bushes, his cart opened partially so he could get at his belongings.

Treyton crept forward and slipped behind the cart. With one arm, he seized the Elf around the neck, while pinning the man's skinny hands behind his back.

"Why are you following me?" Treyton whispered in his ear.

The Elf struggled. "Let me go!"

Treyton tightened his grip. "I'll let you go once you tell me why you're following me."

"Those Garshu would kill me if they found me. It seemed a good idea to leave. I can't help that you are taking the same road as me."

Releasing him, Treyton drew his sword, the steel of his blade cooling the neck of the Elf in seconds.

"Liar."

The Elf straightened at this new threat. He glared at

Treyton, his eyes narrow and spiteful. His build was diminished for an Elf, bony and weak in appearance. His ebony complexion was weathered—an indication that he'd had a hard life in the sun. Behind bright blue eyes, however, there was intelligence.

"Why are you following me?" Treyton demanded. "I'll only ask this last time. I kill to survive, Elf. Do not believe for a moment I would fret over ending you."

The Elf swallowed hard and looked at Treyton's unfaltering, rippling arm as it grasped the sword's hilt.

"I followed you because...you saved my life. I wanted to thank you. I-I am sorry if I have angered you."

Treyton eyed the Elf and decided he was telling the truth. He lowered his arm, sheathing his sword.

"I don't know why I saved your life. You could've had me killed. I should've let you stretch."

The Elf rubbed his reddened neck. "Well, I thank you, nevertheless."

"It's done," Treyton said with a quick shrug. "You told the Garshulan you had a family to look after. Go back to them. Leave me alone."

Without another word, he walked back to his makeshift camp, packed up the pans he had used and rolled his bed. Then he saddled his horse and started down the path toward Follok. It was the first town he would pass on his way to Paraan and the farm.

After a while, he decided to walk on foot. His horse was attracting too many green flies. Before long, he heard the clanking of pots. He whipped his head around and spotted the culprit.

The Elf hobbled not far behind, tirelessly dragging his precious cart.

"I told you to leave me alone!" Treyton hollered.

There was no answer.

Hours passed.

When Treyton emerged from Sorcha Forest, he saw the cottages and buildings of Follok. The town was abuzz with its rebuilding after the Garshu raid. He smiled, even though he was sad at the sight of the community having to restore their homes.

Mounting his horse once again, he passed along the outskirts of Follok, rounding the town rather than going through it. As he began the trek toward Cholart, he glanced over his shoulder and saw the Elf emerging from the Forest. He kicked his horse into a gallop, deciding to spend the night in Cholart, rather than camping out like normal.

He resolved that the Elf would not know of his plan.

Bean staggered toward the farm, fresh cuts on his body. He shoved open the door of the cottage and fell face-first onto the floor at Nell's feet.

"Bean!" she cried.

She scooped up the unconscious, blood-soaked boy.

When Bean awoke several hours later, Nell was sitting beside him, holding his hand. He quickly withdrew it and tried to sit up.

"Bean, be careful," Nell said. "Your back is covered in awful wounds. Well, your whole body is. What happened?"

The concern in her eyes was genuine, tearful.

"I dunno. Please go away." He spoke calmly, yet forcefully and then rolled to his side with a groan.

She hovered in the doorway, watching him until she heard his soft snores. When she turned, Karistaal and Peter were standing in the hall.

Nell tiptoed from the room.

"He won't tell you where he's been," Peter said, shaking his head. "He never does. I have only ever seen him come back like this once before. Otherwise, he usually returns in good spirits, as though he went for a walk through a flower garden."

"And the other time he came back like this?" Nell asked.

"Oh, it was cycles ago," Karistaal said. "It was the first time he had left. Scared the life out of us. We thought he was dead, but instead he came back looking like...*this*. He was only seven cycles old."

The inn that Treyton found in Cholart smelled of manure. A drunken Dwarf woman ran it, so he should have known better than to stop there. He had drawn his hood to conceal his identity, but he knew she saw him. His quarters were a small corner in the attic, a room suitable only for criminals or those in hiding, and the bread and lukewarm soup the woman had thrust into the room was mediocre at best.

Treyton left the bowl at the door and pulled out his own rations. Chewing on a strip of meat, he looked out the window. It gave a good view of the small town, and as the moons rose over the buildings, he allowed his thoughts to wander to less than serious matters.

He watched a young Elf couple sitting at the fountain in the centre of town. A strange emotion crept over him. He straightened, cleared his throat and glanced around the room, as if to make sure no one had witnessed his behaviour.

His eyes drifted back to the couple. The young Elf caressed his love's cheek. She smiled, holding a bouquet of flowers in deep violets and indigos—the same colours as her dress. The Elf boy leaned in for a kiss.

Treyton looked away.

He stared at the cot and saw Nell lying on it. Her crimson hair was incredibly long; the bountiful curls covered intimate parts of her naked body. She signalled him to join her on the bed. Her expression gutted him.

He swallowed, and the vision evaporated. He was shocked. Male Humans did not usually have the gift of vision. That had truly been a blessing from Saros.

Disappointment and confusion consumed him as he glanced out the window again. The couple was gone, retired to a place of privacy. Across the square, the shutters to a large window burst open.

He watched as a candle was lit and moans of intimacy

could be heard. He looked down at the sign labelling the building and decided to close his own shutters.

He did not want to witness the goings on of a brothel house.

The next morning, Treyton set out early, long before the town awoke. The porter had been told of the Human staying upstairs and knew his mistress would want him gone as soon as possible. His relief was evident as he watched Treyton leave.

The sun was coming up on the horizon as Treyton rode toward Paraan. It cast bronze and crimson rays onto the foliage, causing him to think of Nell's hair. He shook the thought from his mind and glanced behind him. For a moment, he thought he saw that infernal Elf, but dismissed it when the path lay empty.

He passed by Paraan quickly, keeping in mind to skirt the town. It was not long before he was on the road where he had first laid eyes on Nell. He remembered the strength she showed when she had spoken forcefully to Liam. Then he thought of the kiss he had witnessed between them.

Distressed and unfocussed, he decided to stop for a moment. He wove his horse through the trees and bushes. Then he jumped down and pulled some bread and water from his bag.

Before long, he was certain he was not alone.

He drew his sword and peered through the bushes.

"That blasted Elf," he hissed under his breath.

The Elf emerged from Paraan's border, his eyes darting all around and his face wearing signs of distress. Following the same path, he passed by Treyton. He muttered quiet curses as he teetered onward with his cart.

When he was gone, Treyton emerged from the bushes, resolved that he would stay off the path and ride through the trees to the farm.

Why is that Elf going to so much trouble to follow me?

Treyton wore the journey's toll as he reached Garick and Nell's lands. It was late morn. No one was in the yard when he secured his horse and gave it water and fresh hay.

He cautiously approached the cottage.

When he entered the kitchen, Nell was kneading bread, and despite their argument from days earlier, she smiled at him, her face spotted with flour and her hair loosely falling from its binding.

Peter stumbled into the kitchen, yawning.

"Ah, you're back!" he said, patting Treyton's shoulder. "Why don't you go wash at the well? I will unpack your things. Be quick though, for we would all like to discuss our journeys. There have been developments."

The old man picked up Treyton's bags and disappeared, leaving a baffled Treyton.

"What developments?" he murmured.

When he entered the sitting room, Lachlin was sitting by the cold hearth, the glow from a nearby window lighting the book in her hand. She looked up, saw him and immediately looked away. A moment later, she rose and propped herself up on the window ledge. Glancing at him one more time, she shimmied out through the space and disappeared.

Confused at her behaviour, Treyton shrugged it off. From the table by the door, he grabbed a towel and a new bar of soap that Nell had compressed last moon. It was made with lavender oils and sprigs of mint.

He headed outside to the well. He sat down along its edge, removed his shirt and gazed at the cottage. Karistaal was in the garden gathering herbs, while Peter tended to the Buktrana. Lachlin had wandered over to the chickens and was spreading feed among them.

It was interesting to watch his family pitching in and managing a household. It was something they had never experienced before. They had been running for so long that the prospect of living normal farming lives filled with normal activities was so foreign.

Normal was foreign.

He stripped down and washed, his mind wandering back to his trip. His journey would be disappointing to everyone.

He thought of the infuriating Elf and made a mental note to let everyone know about him, despite the fact that it was probably for nothing.

As Treyton finished washing, he recalled his vision of Nell at the inn. He wistfully glanced at the cottage, knowing she was inside and oblivious to what he could no longer ignore—his feelings for her.

In the kitchen, Nell was conscious of Liam's presence behind her as she kneaded a batch of bread dough. She stiffened when his hand brushed her lower back.

"Nell," he said. "Kris said she brought up a bag of dyjaars, thinking it was food. Have you seen it?"

"Er...no, I have not."

Liam shrugged, and then left the room.

She stared after him and let out a sigh. They had still not spoken about the night of his drunken fervour. It had nearly slipped her mind in all the excitement. Now that everyone was back at the farm, tending to regular activities, it began to weigh heavily on her.

How different Liam is from Treyton.

She remembered how Treyton had acted in the Sarkian bookshoppe. His behaviour had caught her by surprise. She pictured his broad shoulders and recalled the scent of raw cinnamon on his skin. She was alarmed to find her pulse racing and her forehead dampening at the thought.

She stopped kneading, her flour-coated hands covering her mouth in astonishment. How could she be feeling such things? How could she be feeling such things for two men?

Suddenly, as if by divine intervention, Treyton passed outside the kitchen window. His freshly washed hair was smoothed back. His white tunic was open to the breeze, showing off his tanned, muscular body. He gave Nell a look of yearning and was gone before she could begin to fathom what that look had done to her.

Garick was down in the closet chamber sorting through things with Liam. There was not much said between them, mostly because of Garick's foul mood. Liam had attempted some earlier conversation, but was shot down when the Elf asked him to 'shut his hole'. This had taken Liam by surprise. They had worked in silence ever since, and time passed unbearably slow.

After a few hours, Garick cleared his throat.

"So…I think that we should all discuss our visits over lunch. We really should see where we are, so we can plan things."

Liam was stunned. "Well, I'm a little surprised at your eagerness. I had always thought you were against our rebellion, being so protective of Nell and all. I almost never expected you to return."

Garick absorbed this for a moment.

"I confess I was against this in the beginning," he said finally. "As you say, I am protective of Nell. But for me not to return? Do not forget yourself, Liam. This is *my* home. Besides, several new events have—shall we say—*rekindled* my desire for these plans to proceed." He smiled grimly. "I thirst for the chance to participate."

Liam frowned.

Garick's words were most disturbing.

Chapter Sixteen

"I think it is about time we discussed how everyone's journeys went," Peter said to those seated in the dining hall.

Karistaal and Garick were in the kitchen, with Nell assisting them. They brought out an assortment of breads, meats and cheeses and set them on the table. Famished, they all dug into the meal. Bean sat in the corner of the hall, hungrily stuffing food into his mouth, his plate on his lap.

To Nell's surprise, Garick poured Tartwine into all the glasses. It was his third glass that day. He was becoming a formidable rival for Liam with his indulgences into the wine.

Peter took a hearty gulp. "Liam and I had an interesting visit. I believe it was most successful. In Santz alone, there are remarkable things going on. Liam and I found it extremely difficult to manoeuvre the streets, though, for it is overrun with Garshu."

"Why are there so many?" Nell asked.

"They seem to be amassing their armies," Peter replied, "enslaving the people of the city to make weaponry for them. We went to these *pits* the people feared so, and I have never before laid eyes on some of those swords. The scene was horrible. Elves and Dwarves of all ages were led around on chains and beaten to near death. They were also speaking in a language I have never heard. The only thing I can think of is that it is Garshurian."

Eyebrows went up at this statement, for it had been countless cycles since the ancient tongue of the Garshu had been used.

"Aye," Liam agreed. "The people there are suffering terribly. We'll get many supporters from Santz. I met a young Elvish woman, who I'm confident will spread the news. Oh, and I checked Aldon's old place. It was deserted. Either he has gone or he has fallen victim to the pits."

"The support is good news," Garick said.

With the exception of Liam, all eyes turned to him, the largest pair belonging to Nell. She was about to question Garick's comment when Lachlin interrupted.

"Pandrag was free of Garshu. We were able to practically run a recruiting forum. There were hundreds interested in joining our fight. I'll bet the whole of Pandrag turns out."

Nell nodded. "Yes, we met many citizens who were eager to fight, but there were some who resented our presence."

"And Ronif?" Peter asked.

"We never made it to Ronif. We were on the way, but I decided to come home." She looked apprehensively at Garick. "I had a feeling we should come back early."

Garick ignored her and turned to Treyton. "How was it in the south? Many supporters?"

Treyton shook his head. "I'm afraid I've let you all down. Bryonn was so overrun I wasn't able to make any inquiries. Fairsome was worse. The moment I entered the city, a Dwarf woman somehow recognized me and bellowed to Saros above. The Garshu hung her for her *lies*. Then an Elf saw me. He was to be hung too, but I cut him loose."

"Were you seen?" Lachlin demanded.

"Nay, I was out of that city before the Elf hit the ground. He did follow me, however, into Sorcha Forest. I confronted him and told him to let me be. He ended up following me almost all the way here. I lost him after Paraan."

Everyone gaped at him as though it were his mind he had lost, not the Elf.

"He was harmless," Treyton said dryly. "Gaunt as death. Believe me, we'll never see him again."

No one looked quite convinced.

"I did meet one person I think you'll find quite interesting," he said with a grin. "There is a Withican in Bryonn. What's unusual about her is that she's from a mixed bloodline. Half Elf, half Human."

Forks dropped to plates as everyone stopped eating and brows rose in disbelief. Treyton continued to tell of Deni and her appearance, leaving out the news of her prophecy.

Tuning out the latest revelation, Garick continued eating, until he felt eyes on him. He looked around.

"Garick," Karistaal said hesitantly. "You...uh...haven't told us of your trip. Was it pleasant?"

The Elf looked at her, his eyes aflame.

"Pleasant? No, my dear, it was not. I would rather not speak of it." He scowled. "And I would like it if you would all leave me bloody well alone about it."

He thrust his plate across the table and strode from the room. Somewhere in the cottage, a door slammed.

Those left at the table exchanged uncomfortable glances, until Nell broke the silence.

"He will be tolerated. As my kin, he will be."

There was no further talk.

The morning of the meeting arrived quickly, and Nell was somewhat prepared, though fearful. She was going into battle. Her eyes sought the picture of her mother and she instantly felt better. She studied the graceful, feminine features, knowing she was studying her own.

From under the bed, she retrieved the makeshift sword and laughed at it.

So much had changed. She had certainly advanced.

She thought of that morning, not even a cycle ago, in which she dreamt of glory and daring fights. Only Saros knew what was to come, but she knew it would not be as noble as she imagined.

A feeling of dread washed over her.

"Everything will change after today."

She dressed and emerged from her room. From the doorway, she watched Karistaal and Peter exchange quiet sentiments.

Nell felt very alone.

Will I ever be the recipient of such intimacies?

She peeked at Liam. He was in deep discussion with Garick—something about the Buktrana. They were not arguing, but it was clear each man was irritated.

Treyton stood at the table, packing up some of the food, while Lachlin looked at him, a smile plastered across her face. She laughed wholeheartedly at something he said, and it occurred to Nell that she had never seen Lachlin look like that before.

Treyton grinned too, but his eyes found their way over to Nell. When he caught her gaze, his smile vanished and he gave her a strange look—one Nell recognized from the day he had returned.

Lachlin's cheerful mood evaporated when she saw Treyton watching Nell. The scowl that had become prominent lately, returned to her face and she completed her tasks with deliberate vigour.

Nell gave Treyton a nod, then slipped from the room.

Footsteps sounded behind her.

"Are you ready?" Garick asked, unsmiling.

"You let me sleep," she complained.

She decided she was going to meet his new nastiness with an equal manner.

He let out a grunt. "I did not think of you. You are old enough to get up on your own accord."

She reddened at the insult.

"Garick, what happened?" she asked, placing a hand on his arm. "You have come back to me a different person. Please tell me what happened. Did you find your family?"

Garick refused to look at her.

"Listen carefully," he said, sliding a hand into his pocket. "I do not want to talk about my trip. Do not ask me again." He pulled away and strode outside.

Nell watched him go, her heart pounding.

The town of Paraan had become overrun with a multitude of visitors. Tents and temporary shelters were erected on the outskirts. As the Humans and Garick approached, the populace emerged from their dwellings. It started with a young Elf who cheered at the sight of them, and soon became a thunderous welcome.

They rode into Paraan with families marching behind them, warrior farmers raising their arms in salute, and Elvish women hanging out their windows, throwing flowers at them for luck.

It was a noble scene.

Nell felt immense joy, while Lachlin appeared confused, yet she kept riding, erect and dignified. Liam and Treyton energetically shook hands across their saddles, and Peter and Karistaal waved, overwhelmed by the hordes that gathered. Only Garick seemed on guard, his eyes scavenging the streets for any Garshu.

In the town square, they dismounted at the platform.

As Treyton silenced the crowd, Nell surveyed the faces of those who volunteered their services—and probably their lives. There were easily thousands upon thousands of people, a diverse wave of Elves and Dwarves of all shapes and sizes. The horde cheered, their encouraging faces looking to the Humans for guidance and leadership. It was as Treyton had said—they were leading the citizens again, like in the stories.

All of a sudden, Nell noticed the uniformed men in the crowd. They were scattered throughout the gathering. She squinted at the insignia on one of the sashes. Nine tulips were emblazoned across it.

Her heart leapt at the sight.

She leaned over to Lachlin. "Look! Controlice."

Lachlin whispered to Peter of the presence of Controlice, the former enforcing presence of Cantro.

A murmur flowed through the crowd until it became widely known that there were still Controlice around. Their skills would be extremely helpful.

"Silence, please!" Treyton called out.

He quieted the townspeople as much as he could, but many were excited at the prospect of fighting back. Even more were anxious to begin fighting. There was a renewed vigour to avenge the deaths of families and friends who had perished at the hands of the Garshu.

"People of Cantro," Treyton said in a strong voice. "I can see word has travelled far and wide of our rebellion. Saros is certainly watching us from above to allow such good fortune in such a treacherous time."

The crowd cheered, some raising their hands to Saros.

"We have an idea to destroy the Garshu," Liam cut in. "We'd like to share it with you now."

He proceeded to pass on Nell's plan for wiping out the Garshulas, but it was clear that many did not agree with it.

"What of the Dukev?" one Dwarf demanded. "They will slaughter any that near the nests."

"We'll meet the Dukev head on, if they exist," Treyton countered.

This motivated some, while others shook their heads and whispered their objections. People began to stir restlessly.

Nell's face wrinkled in dismay.

They were beginning to lose support.

She stepped forward. "Do you see who Saros has brought us?"

The crowd buzzed with surprise as the uniformed men strode toward the platform. Nell counted thirty Controlice. There was once that many in every small town. This disheartened her, but she wore a confident grin nonetheless. They were an omen—a signal of forgotten strength and control, in a world that has lost everything.

And *that* made Nell feel empowered.

The Controlice looked at the Humans and saluted them with their ritual gesture—a quick process of holding out their spears in front and pounding them into the ground while stomping their right foot.

Nell glanced at Peter. His eyes pooled with tears at the honour of the Controlice salute. He whispered something to Karistaal and she grasped his hand. Peter was old enough to remember the Controlice, to remember the authority they once wielded.

Treyton nudged Nell. "That was quick thinking to point them out."

Garick rudely pushed Treyton aside. "Cantronians! I am Garick of the Shanasar Clan. I owe all my pain and rage to the Garshu. They have taken everything from me. They have taken everything from you too. Will you now listen to us?"

The crowd hushed.

"I implore you to lend us your vengeance," Garick said. "We shall grow so mighty as one that we will smite the Garshu with a passion and retribution such as they have never seen before. Let us be one, Cantronians. Fight!"

The townspeople joined in. "Fight! Fight!"

Nell gaped at Garick, stunned. The look of fierce reprisal that fuelled his eyes made her shiver. She followed her friends away from the platform, toward a tent that the Controlice had set up. The crowd dispersed somewhat, but for the most part, they followed in mass numbers, unsure of what to do next.

Treyton mumbled something to one of the senior ranking Controlice. Then he jogged back to the platform.

"I bid you listen!" he bellowed. "All those faithful to Saros and the Cantronian way of life, please do the following. There are tents set up in the four corners of town, and at the entrance and exit of the square. Register at one so an infantry can be formed and our attack plan confirmed."

The people now were moving in some order.

Liam grabbed Nell by the arm. "Can you take the booth at the exit? Be sure to tell them where to camp and which battalion they are in."

She smiled. "Finally trusting me with something, eh?"

His brow arched. "Actually, it's because you're one of the few who can write well."

He left her standing there, feeling foolish. She stormed off to the exit tent where a huge line-up was already amassing. There were five Controlice waiting for her. One handed her a stack of pages and some sticks of compressed coal.

"It's all we have," he said.

"This is much cruder than I am used to," she said, "but it will do."

Nell's hand began to cramp as the sun lowered to eye level. She leaned out of the tent and peered down the line. Scores of people went on far into the distance. It looked as if they had gathered at the town square, taking whatever line opened up first. Her gaze swept across town, but she could not make out who was running the tent at the entrance.

A scrawny Elf was next in line.

"Name please," she said.

The Elf kept his head lowered. "Dintik."

"What is your Clan, Elf?" Impatience crept into her voice.

"Unknown."

Nell stared at him, noting his ragged clothes and tightly drawn hood. She could not make out his face. She thought she should investigate further, since an Elf not knowing his Clan was quite uncommon, but she could see that her line-up had dwindled. There were only a few left to register.

She let her fatigue get the better of her. "Camp on the southern outskirts, soldier. Welcome to Battalion Five."

The Elf shuffled away.

The next in line was a young Elf woman. She had a wide smile plastered onto her face.

"I told Liam I would tell people," she said excitedly. "Is he here?"

Distracted, Nell looked over her shoulder and saw the Elf she had just registered. As he dragged a cart over to the campsite, he glanced back at her, and then quickly looked away.

However, it was too late. She had seen his face, his eyes.

"So do you know where Liam is?" the girl asked again.

Nell dismissed thoughts of the Elf and turned to the girl. "Sorry, I have no idea. Try the town square."

When the girl had left, she finished with the remaining Dwarfs and Elves in the line. Afterward, she stood, relieved, and stretched her aching muscles. She could not resist surveying the town, but saw no sign of the strange Elf or his cart. Gathering the registration papers, she made her way across the square.

She could not get the Elf's eyes out of her mind.

Why do they seem so familiar? Do I know him?

Chapter Seventeen

"Good sir, may I have a moment of your time?"

Turning, Peter was met with a worn, brown cloak. His eyes traveled upward, past massive hands resting on a well-fed belly, until they met the face of a Giant. Shaggy grey hair fell down the Giant's back and his eyes danced with an almost childlike fervour.

"Of course," Peter answered politely.

The Giant gave Peter an unexpectedly sophisticated grin. "I am here as ambassador for both Giant settlements. Travelling right now is such a trying thing that I came alone. We wish to express our joy at the idea of a rebellion against the Garshu. Although we will not wield a weapon, we wish to offer our healing services, should any of your warriors require such a thing."

Peter nodded. "Thank you. It is too bad you will not fight. With your stature, you would certainly give us an advantage."

"It is against our beliefs, sir. We are healers and peacekeepers. Violence is foreign to us, except for its effects." The Giant sighed. "We are far too familiar with that."

Peter offered a hand. "I'm Peter Winton Coresani. We welcome your alliance."

The Giant shook his hand gently and then smiled. "In your tongue, I am called Odorff. We will do what we can to aid you."

Now that Nell had been to Pandrag, she had another town against which to compare the smaller Paraan's features. The brickwork on the buildings was quite lovely, as were the soft scented wildflowers that grew between the houses and businesses.

As she passed a charred section of town, she recalled the violent day when the Garshu had visited. It occurred to her that none had shown up today. She had half-expected that once word of the rebellion had circulated, at least one Garshulan would come to inspect the rumour.

A feeling of uneasiness suddenly consumed her. She spun around, examining her surroundings a little more closely. Her sword's cool hilt rested against her palm. She turned again, the feeling overwhelming her as her eyes darted from building to building. When she saw nothing out of the ordinary, she calmed herself.

Then she saw Liam. He was walking toward her and she noted that her stomach did not clench at the sight of him.

This is good.

She headed for him, removing her hand from her sword.

"How was it?" he asked, gesturing to the tent in which she had spent most of the day.

"Long, I suppose. Is everyone else done registering?"

"Aye," Liam said. "You look tired. Are you all right?"

Nell raised her eyebrows. "I am fine. My mind is running away with me, that is all." She paused. "Do you find it strange that not one Garshulan came today? That with all the villages we contacted, not one heard of the rebellion? I find it odd."

Liam considered this for a moment.

"Well, I suppose," he said, sounding a bit unsure. "I hadn't thought of it. I was preoccupied with all the organization. Have you seen anything that you think should warrant our attention?"

She shook her head, frowning. "Everyone was either very eager, or very angry. There was only one Elf that was slightly suspicious, but I think he was an orphan. He did not have a Clan name. There was something so…*familiar* about him. In his eyes."

Liam nodded, lost in thought.

Nell regretted having to add to everything he already had on his mind, but she was glad she had mentioned her concerns about the Garshu.

"Let's go to *The Cantro Cavern*," Liam suggested.

The Cantro Cavern was an underground pub near the outskirts of town. When they entered, the bar was packed with customers, and there was barely room to breathe. The barkeep's satisfied grin was unmistakable. Business was booming.

Liam and Nell squeezed into two empty seats at the bar. Then they spun around to survey the room. It was full of inebriated would-be warriors and farmer-soldiers talking bravely to each other, but sounding ridiculous and naive.

"I'll kill the Garshu with my bare hands," an Elf slurred.

Liam leaned over to Nell. "I think we need a drink."

Bean and Peter entered one of the inns on the east side of the square. Garick had agreed that they had more than enough currency to treat the entire group to a nice evening at an inn, rather than sleeping outdoors as usual. It would be a new experience for most of them. Bean was especially excited, since it was his suggestion in the first place.

"Meals made for us and our beds ain't gonna have bugs," he said to Peter as they approached the Dwarf woman at the desk. "And a hot bathhouse spring. We're Gods today!"

"We'll need at least three rooms, four if you have them," Peter told the woman. "For tonight and maybe tomorrow night."

The woman gave an eager nod. "Last four available.

We're actually going to be full up for the first time in cycles. They're yours if you've got the currency."

Peter raised an eyebrow. "How much?"

"Four dyjaars for the lot," the Dwarf told him.

Peter dropped the coins onto the desk.

The woman scooped them up and gave him a toothy grin. Then she led them up the creaky staircase, all the way to the top. When they reached the last step, she pointed to three doors on one side of the hall and one door at the end.

"The keys are all in the door handles. Just leave them there when you're ready to leave."

Peter and Bean inspected the rooms. They were small but satisfactory.

"Help me with our belongings," Peter said.

Returning to their horses, they unloaded weapons and bags, and moved them into the rooms. Since the others in their group were still busy, they unloaded their horses too.

"I'll share with Garick," Bean volunteered, as he dropped a bag on the bed.

This surprised Peter. The Elf's change in attitude had put him at a distance from everyone.

They emerged from the inn and found Lachlin sitting on the steps.

She glanced up, bleary-eyed. "Are we are settled, then?"

Peter cocked his head. "Are you all right, love?"

"I'm *fine*!" She indicated a nearby pub. "Liam and Nell are in there. Shall we join them?" She gritted her teeth.

Peter and Bean exchanged uneasy looks.

Inside *The Cantro Cavern*, they were stunned by the chaotic atmosphere. Patrons were eager to show off their fighting skills and they squabbled like birds.

"There they are," Bean said, pointing at the bar.

Liam noticed them and waved. "Ah, hello! Join us for a drink. Where's Kris?" He stumbled over the words, his heavy intoxication embarrassingly obvious.

Nell swivelled on the stool, her face red with discomfort. She was relieved to see Peter, Bean and Lachlin, and she slid to another stool, allowing Lachlin to sit down between beside her brother.

Nell nudged Lachlin. "Does he always get like this when he drinks ale?"

Lachlin frowned. "Like what?"

Before Nell could answer, Liam leaned across his sister's lap and gazed at her longingly, his posture wavering.

Nell raised her eyebrows. "Like that."

Ignoring her, Lachlin caught sight of the drink that the barkeep had placed in front of her. She sighed. Then she threw the ale down her throat, not stopping until the glass was empty.

Everyone gawked at her in surprise.

"Nicely done, sister," Liam slurred.

Standing abruptly, Lachlin dropped a few sanaars on the bar. She glanced once more at Liam and Nell, a mix of anger and jealousy on her face. Mumbling something incoherent, she snatched the empty glass and stomped toward the door. Without warning, she let out a fierce scream and threw the glass at the wall. It shattered into a storm of furious shards, but she marched through them.

Then she was gone.

"Well, what a brazen one," Liam mumbled.

He reached for his glass, but failed to grab it. Instead, he fell backwards, slid off the stool and passed out on the floor. Peter hauled him up, muttering curses while he and Bean dragged him out of the pub.

"Are you coming back to the inn?" Peter asked Nell once they were all outside.

"Nay, I am going to find Garick. I have not seen him all day."

She set off toward the entrance to Paraan, while Peter and Bean hauled an unconscious Liam to the inn.

"How about these?" Treyton asked, holding out a handful of pretty, if not gangly, weeds.

Karistaal clucked. "Treyton, my love…when I said bring her flowers, I meant it." She took the weeds from his hand and replaced them with yellow posies. "Now, I want you to be yourself, but be a prince. Talk to the girl, but listen to her also."

Treyton nodded nervously.

He had asked Karistaal an hour ago to help him and ended up spilling all his woes to her. He finally admitted to her—*and* to himself—that he had feelings for Nell. Once he said it, he was astonished at the sense of relief that washed over him. Karistaal had then proceeded to give him advice on courting Nell.

He walked awkwardly to the exit of Paraan, glancing back at Karistaal for encouragement.

"Tell her how you feel!" she yelled, waving him on.

She smiled, one hand on her hip. *Young love…*

Suddenly, she felt the sensation of being watched. Glancing to one side, she saw a teary Lachlin standing in the darkness, her arms crossed over her chest.

"How could you?" Lachlin sobbed, her voice full of pain.

Karistaal was at a loss for words. She stared at Lachlin, then at Treyton's retreating back, and then to Lachlin once more.

It became clear.

"Oh, my darling. I had no idea."

She moved towards Lachlin with open arms, but the girl swatted them away.

"Don't touch me! You must have known." Lachlin pointed to Treyton's distant form. "He's the only man I've ever known that wasn't my brother! Surely you must have thought that I…that he…" She bit back more tears, then shook her head. "It's no matter. He loves Nell. There's no room for me." She shuffled away, dejected.

"Lachlin, I'm so—"

"Leave me be, Kris! I want to be alone." Lachlin stifled another sob. "I've always been alone."

The nagging feeling that tugged at the corner of Nell's

mind would not cease. There was something strange about the Garshu not coming through Paraan at all that day. Wrapped in her thoughts, she realized she had stopped in her tracks.

"Nell!" someone called.

Garick stood a few steps away. If she had not heard him speak, she never would have recognized him. The shadows on his face darkened his usually kind eyes and the creases in his skin made him look hollow, sedated.

"Garick," she said, eyeing him with caution. "I was looking for you. I have not seen you all day."

His expression remained blank.

She saw that the night actually had very little to do with his appearance. His pallor was milky, and the way he looked at her made her shiver.

"Well, what do you want?" he retorted.

She frowned.

She should have been prepared for his new attitude.

"I need to talk to you, Garick. I know you told me not to ask you about it, but I need to know what happened with your family. Your entire manner has changed. You are dark and unpleasant. I am worried about you. Please...talk to me."

Garick's demeanour did not change, but she was certain she saw a fire in his eyes, a blaze stoked by her words.

"You are so naïve," he said bitterly. "You have not experienced anything. I have sheltered you from every terror-filled thing in this entire world."

He leaned in so close that she smelled the sour stink of stale wine exuding from his pores.

"You found out your parents were murdered years ago," he said, "but you never witnessed their death. You did not walk into your home after thirteen cycles to find your parents' corpses defiled and stinking like rotten fruit. You did not find that after making a decision that you had no choice about, your own father despised ever conceiving you."

His lower lip curled in a disdainful sneer. "Do you

know what it is like to have your very roots torn from you? No! The most traumatic thing to ever happen to you was so long ago you do not even remember it. How sickeningly lucky!"

He scowled at her until the hairs on the back of her neck stood erect.

"You know nothing of pain," he added. "Of strife. Of regret."

Tears welled in Nell's eyes and spilled down her cheeks.

Garick let out a sound of disgust. "Now, do not try to tug on my heartstrings the way you did when your parents were slaughtered. You did enough to me then. You asked me what happened with my family. I told you. *You* asked for the truth."

She whimpered, her head swimming from his cruel words. "Garick, I—"

"Leave me alone, girl!"

The sight of his indifferent back made Nell sob.

"Please, Garick…"

The Elf spun around. "*What?*"

"I am so sorry," she wept.

"Oh, yes, you are. Though sorry does not bring my mother back from the dead. Sorry does not clear my father's thoughts about me. Sorry does not tell me where my brothers and sisters are—if they have been sold into Garshu slavery, if they are hurt or even alive."

He panted heavily as he stared into the distance.

"Sorry does not fill the emptiness that is eating me whole. But do you know what will?" A thin smile crept onto his face. "I will butcher a hundred Garshu for every cycle I was away from my family."

Nell gasped, stunned by his ruthless longing.

Garick's smile grew into a fierce grin and his eyes glazed over with unholy delight. "I will tear into their flesh and make them feel the pain they have caused so many." His hands reached into the air for an enemy that only his frenzied vision could see. "I will cause them such anguish that they will be begging me to end their worthless life, just so they can be relieved of me."

Horrified by his words, Nell backed away slowly and then ran with all her might.

Chapter Eighteen

"Nell!" Treyton hollered.

He watched Nell sprint across the square, her hair shining in the moonlight, like fire tracing the air.

He called her name again, but to no avail. She either was ignoring him or did not hear his desperate cries. The flowers fell to the ground and his hopes drifted away with them.

What was I thinking?

Resigned, he vanished into the night.

Nell ran as fast as her legs would permit. She knew they would never carry her away fast enough. She thought of Garick. She did not know who that Elf was in his place, but it was not her guardian.

He is not my beloved Garick!

She sobbed harder, remembering the cruel, alien look in his eyes. Those were not the kind eyes that softened at the sound of her laughter. She pictured his hands finding an invisible Garshulan to strangle. Those were not the gentle hands that had lifted her from the gravel when she skinned her knees playing with the chickens.

Most horrifying, however, was Garick's 'smile'. His lips showed pure ecstasy at the thought of maiming another. He had never harmed anyone—not even a Garshulan.

That devilish crevice was not the same that had sealed a thousand nights rest with a soft kiss.

No, that face—that Elf—was foreign to her.

Grief-stricken, she skidded to a stop, threw her arms in the air and flung back her head.

"What happened?" she screamed at the skies. "Saros! What did you do to him?"

She doubled over in distress and sank to the ground, her limbs aching. When she could sob no longer, she lay in silence, a constant sheet of tears blinding her. In the quiet, she heard her ragged breathing, an owl in the distance, raucous friends at a tavern, and a fountain not far away.

Then, footsteps growing closer.

A shadow blocked the moonlight. It leaned down and lifted her from the earth, gathering her in strong arms.

Nell drifted into an exhausted sleep.

I've always been alone.

Lachlin ran with all her might. There was no direction to her erratic scurry, for she ran from Karistaal, from Treyton, from Nell and from the Merfolk. She ran from everything her whole life had granted and denied her. Mostly, she ran from herself.

Finally collapsing in the grass, she raised her head and her watery vision fell on a bench monument in front of her.

"Shirell?"

The sculpture gazed down at her, its stone eyes alarmingly real.

Lachlin studied her surroundings.

"Where in Paraan am I?"

She turned back to the statue, surprised that there were still erections of Shirell in existence. It *was* a sculpture of the First Human—she was not mistaken. The woman's body was bent slightly, one hand reaching down in offering.

Lachlin stroked the outstretched hand, and then

placed her damp cheek on its palm. Her heart skipped a beat, for she found the carving warm and reassuring. What happened next was amazing.

The next morning, Lachlin awoke in her bed at the inn feeling more positive—even cheerful. She never bothered to go looking for the statue, for she knew she wouldn't find it.

She knew what had happened.

"Shirell herself has come to me."

This extraordinary fact changed Lachlin's outlook on everything. She courageously accepted Treyton's choice. She decided that she needed to focus more on the upcoming battle with the Garshu, than on herself. She knew Shirell was watching over her.

"Shh...Nell."

A soothing voice brought Nell back to the present. She peeled her eyes open, only to find her vision blurred. She felt a cool cloth on her forehead and a warm hand clasped around her own.

She blinked and Treyton's face came into view. He was obviously worried, yet she could not remember when *she* last felt more relieved.

"You were dreaming, I think," he said.

Sitting in a chair beside her, he wiped the cloth across her brow once again. As he moved away to wet it in a nearby basin, she caught his scent—mint and lavender.

"You smell good," she blurted. "Like fresh herbs."

He smiled. "Well, luckily I know a pretty girl who makes a decent soap bar."

Nell blushed. She had never been called pretty before.

Doubt suddenly crossed her drowsy mind.

"You do mean me, do you not?"

Treyton chuckled softly and nodded, his eyes sparkling.

She had a peculiar lump in her throat.

Nell struggled to sit up and he came to her aid, fluffing the pillow behind her back. She was on a cot in a cramped storage room lined with shelves of tiny jars. Their labels stated that they were stuffed with various herbs and powders.

Treyton shifted in the chair. "The woman who runs this inn led me here when I asked for help. I thought it would give us more privacy than your room."

Nell gave him a sideways glance.

"I wanted to talk to you," he said, as if reading her thoughts. "I saw you earlier, after your talk with Garick. You ran off when I was about to give you these." From beside the cot he pulled out a drooping bouquet of lemon-coloured wildflowers.

Nell shyly inhaled the sweet scent.

"I called out to you several times," Treyton said. "I thought perhaps you were ignoring me, so I dropped the flowers and began to walk away. Then it was like Saros dropped a stone on me." He gave her a wry smile. "You were so obviously upset, no wonder you did not turn around. You had not heard me. Besides, if I was going to see you about matters such as…well…these, then who was I to just walk away and leave you like that? So I picked the flowers up and ran after you."

She swallowed hard, somehow finding her voice. "And what matters were you coming to see me about?" It came out in a high-pitched squeak.

Treyton moved closer. "I need to tell you something, Nell. Something I've had a hard time realizing, but now that I do, I feel…rejuvenated. But before I do, I need to ask you one question. That kiss I saw between you and Liam—"

"He kissed me. And I wish he had not. He was drunk."

"Of course." Treyton murmured, relieved. He leaned over until his forehead touched hers and he squeezed her hand. The heat of his grasp did not waver. Instead, it burned with a fervour that told her they were never meant to part.

Nell closed her eyes, feeling the emotional intimacy of

their connection. In that moment, she experienced the sapling of love expanding within her, stretching its branches throughout every limb. Her chest grew tight. Her arms and legs were almost numb. Her body yearned for his.

A single tear trickled down her cheek.

She thought her heart might burst. In this simple yet extraordinary moment, she had found everything she had ever needed in this one simple man. He was more than her soul mate. They had been born to experience this priceless gift—to complete each others very being.

"Nell…" Treyton's voice was like a dream. "I lo—"

The door swung open and slammed against the wall.

In the doorway, Garick frowned, surprised to find Nell and Treyton alone in the room.

And holding hands.

He walked toward the bed. "Nell, I have been looking for you all morning. I did not realize you were spending the night in here with Treyton."

His gaze snapped back to Treyton as he reached out a hand to help Nell from the cot.

"No," she said, shaking her head.

Garick shrugged. "Lachlin told me you did not go to your room. Have you been here all night?"

"How is that *your* concern? You do not care if I live or die, let alone disappear without checking in with anyone. After you spoke to me so harshly last night, I fell sick."

She met Treyton's eyes. "Treyton took care of me by bringing me here to mend my cuts from the gravel. He cooled my fever and watched over me while I slept. And once I woke this morning, he assisted me in getting my bearings."

"How considerate of him," Garick muttered.

"It *was* very considerate of him," she said. "He stayed awake all night and tended to me, rather than waking the others and worrying them. So many people can be cruel and hurtful. It is nice to know that there are still some people in Cantro who are willing to help another."

With bitter fury, Nell shoved back the blanket and

stumbled to her feet, unaware of the flowers that fell to the floor. She pushed past a flustered Treyton and stormed out of the room, leaving Garick with his mouth agape and his heart heavy.

Treyton flicked him an irritated look, then disappeared.

Garick stared at the trampled flowers at his feet, feeling anger and sadness at their presence.

A faint murmuring woke Lachlin. She slipped out of bed and crept across the room. Turning the handle carefully, she pulled the heavy door slightly ajar.

Treyton and Nell stood in the hallway, speaking in low, undecipherable tones. They were holding hands. Treyton's face was plastered with a boyish grin, and the joy in his eyes could not be mistaken as he stared at Nell.

Lachlin had never seen him so happy.

She returned to bed, exhausted. Garick had woken her before dawn, demanding to know where Nell was. He had stunk of ale and looked terrible. When she told him that Nell had not come to bed, he stormed off.

Lachlin was sure she would fall asleep in no time. She curled up in the woollen blankets, her back to the door. When it clicked open a few minutes later, she squeezed her eyes shut.

She heard Nell tiptoe into the room. The girl moved quietly toward the bed. Lachlin could feel her burning gaze. Then the blankets were tugged over Lachlin's back and a hand tenderly patted the warm bedspread.

The door opened again, then closed.

Lachlin's eyes fluttered open and she stared at the earthen wall. "What a nice girl."

She frowned. "How I hate her."

Nell rested her head against the wooden ledge of the bathhouse spring. She soaked there now, after enjoying an invigorating scrub bath. Treyton had paid the innkeeper for both of them to indulge. Then he headed off to the male side, leaving her to relax and reflect.

She was in total ecstasy. It was the most surreal and wonderful feeling to have sizzling water bubble all around her.

She was just about to drift off when the door creaked.

A cloaked Karistaal walked in.

She gave Nell a lovely smile, then strolled over to the reservoir that joined the spring. She drew hot water from it and filled a tub. Then she pulled off the cloak, revealing a body that was obviously quite striking once upon a time, but now wore the toils of age.

Nell lowered her eyes in respect until Karistaal had submerged her nakedness in the tub.

Karistaal pulled out a soap bar that Nell had given her before the group had left the farm.

"Treyton tells me your soap is unequalled," she said. "I wanted to try it."

She began to wash, and Nell leaned her head back again, closing her eyes and grinning at the very sound of his name.

Karistaal's voice interrupted her thoughts.

"I can tell you, I've seen that smile before."

Nell's eyes flashed open, bewildered. "What?"

Karistaal snorted. "I said I've seen that smile before—I have. It has been a long time since I have seen it, but I know it well. The last time I saw it was before the Garshu came. Peter and I had our lovely cottage, and in the bedroom was a gilded mirror that my mother had given me on our wedding day. Peter had come in the bedroom to give me a kiss. There was no rhyme or reason for it. It was just because he loved me." She sighed softly, remembering.

"When he turned to leave, I walked over to the window and began to pull back the drapes. As I tied the second one open, I caught a glimpse of my reflection in the mirror beside the window. I wore the same exultant smile you have right now. It happened because of love. It blossomed because, for that short moment, Saros let me feel utter joy."

Karistaal rose gracefully from the tub and headed for the springs. She sank into the water across from Nell.

"So when I say I know that smile," she said with a wink, "I do." She tilted her head back and sighed.

Nell shook her head in amazement. Then she leaned back once more, letting out an equally content sigh.

Chapter Nineteen

"We wondered when you were going to grace us with your presence," Peter said dryly to a semi-comatose Liam.

He pulled out a chair and Liam slumped down, hungover and pale. When he offered the young man some bread, Liam groaned and rested his head on the table.

At the other end, Bean snickered.

Peter's mouth thinned. "You know you need to stop this nonsense, Liam. Anytime you get near ale, you can't seem to stop drinking until you're too drunk to hold your own head up." He leaned closer. "I had to carry your arse back here last night. And I'll tell you, I won't be doing that again anytime soon."

He gave Liam a playful wallop on the back.

Liam let out a loud moan.

"Oh, quit your whining," Peter scolded. "Have some food. You should know by now what gets rid of those morning shakes. Here, have some bread and drink some of the innkeeper's strong tea."

Liam dragged his grey face from the table and slowly began devouring the meal. Soon, colour started to peek into the corners of his skin.

Lachlin descended the stairs. Seeing Peter, she walked over to the table.

Bean pulled out a chair for her.

"Why, thank you, Bean," she said.

The boy took a deep breath. "We wondered when you were going to grace us with your presence, Lachlin. Here, have some bread and drink some of the innkeeper's strong tea."

Repeating the words that Peter had welcomed Liam with, he slid the plate of bread toward her, then handed her a cup of tea.

Peter ruffled the boy's hair. "Good lad."

Lachlin reached for the bowl of fruit in the middle of the table. She took a piece and set it beside her plate. Then she flashed a worried look at Liam.

"How are you feeling, brother?"

Liam grunted, still stuffing his face.

With a sigh, Lachlin took a bite of bread, and then washed it down with the tea. She tore into the peel of the oval fruit, cracking open the slices inside. She offered the fruit to the others, after cramming a juicy piece into her mouth.

Peter and Bean stared at her.

Lachlin had not eaten this vigorously in several moons. She smiled.

That sent them reeling.

When was the last time Lachlin had smiled?

Peter and Bean exchanged wide-eyed looks. Then they shrugged and left Lachlin to her own devices.

She ate happily, staring off into the distance.

Nell emerged from the bathhouse, recharged. She was wrapped in one of the towel cloaks as Karistaal had been. Her damp hair was slicked back, scented with wildflower oil.

When Treyton saw her, he grinned. "You look much more relaxed. I'm glad you're feeling better."

She took his arm, and he led her upstairs to her room, before heading to his own to dress. When she entered the room, she was surprised to discover that Lachlin's bed was empty. The woman had been fast asleep when Nell had left earlier.

Nell quickly changed into what had become her usual attire—a long tunic and pants. She dragged a brush through her wet hair, fluffing it a little so it would dry faster.

She caught sight of her reflection in the mirror. Her eyes gleamed a mint lustre and her cheeks were a rosy pink. Her lips were a bit dry, from the sun and dust. She licked them slowly. Then she recalled Karistaal's story. She felt a little self-conscious. This was the first time she had ever really studied herself in the mirror.

"Do I look attractive?" she whispered.

She had never before been anxious over wanting to be pretty and presentable. She waved off her stressful doubts, telling herself that Treyton had—beyond a doubt—seen her at her very worst last night.

He is not just attracted to my appearance.

She ran the brush through her hair once more, just for good measure. With one last glance in the mirror, she swung open the bedroom door, stepped out into the hall and headed for Treyton's room.

She felt almost liberated. She knew she was maturing and in control of her life, despite what Garick had said to her.

She knocked on the door. It opened slowly, revealing a dressed and grinning Treyton. She studied him for a moment, wondering how she had ever let so much time go by without realizing how she felt.

Treyton embraced her, his body warm against hers.

Then they headed downstairs to eat.

Breakfast was brief, for just as Treyton and Nell joined the group, a ragged-looking Dwarf barged into the dining hall, bloodied and barely alive. He stood in the doorway, gazed at the table of Humans, then crumpled to the floor, blood gushing from wounds to his legs and chest.

Stunned by the unexpected visitor, everyone raced to his side, the Dwarven innkeeper not far behind. Liam and Treyton drew their swords at once and moved to the door.

"*Corin!*" the innkeeper screamed, kneeling next to her husband. "Oh, Corin. What's happened?"

The Dwarf raised a trembling hand to his wife's cheek as tears fell from her eyes onto his bloodstained clothes. Then, with great effort, he swivelled his head.

"Humans, they're here. Ye've been betrayed by one of yer own, I fear. Ye must save us all. Ye must save Cantro." He groaned deeply, and then turned to his wife who was now sobbing uncontrollably. "Caitla, I love ye. By Saros, I love ye, wife. I..." A painful gurgle rattled in his throat as he passed from the world.

Caitla slumped over her dead husband, filling the room with howling, delirious cries of grief.

Nell gazed at Karistaal, an expression of fear and confusion in her eyes.

"He's dead," Karistaal announced.

Nell's hand rested firmly on the hilt of her sword.

"Where was he?" she demanded. "What location did he just come from? Ask his wife."

Karistaal crouched down next to the weeping woman and whispered something in her ear. Caitla hiccupped several words, and then burst into tears.

Karistaal faced the group. "Caitla said he was not in bed last night. She says we should check the home of the tailor's daughter. I think she said her name was Arenel."

"*Arenel the whore!*" Caitla screamed, her eyes red and swollen.

"Let's go," Liam suggested.

Everyone—with the exception of the innkeeper's wife—filed out of the room and headed for the front door. When they stepped outside, all of Paraan was unearthly quiet.

"What's going on?" Bean asked nervously.

"Split up!" Liam shouted. "Bean, stay here in case Garick comes looking for us. Treyton, you and Peter go left. I'll go right with Lachlin. Check with the townsfolk. Find out what's happened. Kris, you take Nell and find the tailor's daughter. Use our signal if you find anything."

They swiftly separated.

Nell's stomach fluttered. "What is the signal, Karistaal?"

"You'll see when I use it, or hear it if someone else does." Karistaal sounded upset.

Nell followed her as she scurried up the steps of a dilapidated cottage. The older Human thumped on the door with the force of a Giant.

An Elf peered out from a peephole, bleary-eyed and half asleep. "What do you want, stranger?"

"I apologize most remorsefully, sir," Nell said. "We are in dire need of directions. We seek the way to the tailor. Would you be most kind as to inform us of the route?"

The Elf raised his eyebrows. "It is far too early for such manners. Go toward the exit gates." He slammed the peephole shut.

Nell hastily descended the stairs, with Karistaal not far behind. They ran in the direction of the gates, arriving at them in mere moments.

"There!" Nell pointed to the wooden sign hanging over a doorway. "The tailor's shop. They must live here too."

They were about to step inside when they heard a great bellow. To Nell, it sounded like the deep inhalation of the old Buktrana back at the farm.

"That's Liam," Karistaal said with dismay. "He's behind this row of buildings. We must go to him."

Nell followed her, amazed at the woman's ability to determine Liam's location just from a single sound.

As they rounded the corner, they came to an alley. At the far end, Lachlin gestured for them to hurry. Nell and Karistaal sprinted down the alley. When they reached Lachlin, Karistaal was panting, out of breath.

"Here, Kris," Lachlin said, leading the woman to an uprooted tree. "Sit for a moment."

"Where's Liam?" Nell asked.

"He sent me outside to meet you," Lachlin said solemnly. "Treyton and Peter are inside with him. It's horrible."

Nell's eyes wandered to a decrepit building.

What dreadful event had occurred?

Soon, Peter stumbled outside, his face pale. He slumped beside Karistaal and placed an arm around her quivering shoulders.

"It was a massacre," he said in an unsteady voice. "There's nothing and no one left in one piece. Most of them were our soldiers, I think. There were about twenty in there, although it's hard to tell from the carnage. They were undoubtedly slaughtered by the Garshu."

Nell's chest tightened with panic.

Garshu! They had been here!

However, one thing did not make sense to her.

"Why does *this* building hold such massacre?" she asked, perplexed. "The innkeeper—Caitla—said her husband was at the *tailor's* place."

Eyes lifted as they each realized the same thing.

"Let's go!" Lachlin said.

"Do you know where the tailor's home is, Nell?" Peter asked.

She nodded. "Karistaal and I were about to inquire there when we heard Liam's signal."

Peter turned to his wife. "Darling, you stay here. Wait for Liam and Treyton, and lead them to the tailor's home. Nell, show Lachlin and I this building. Now."

He followed Nell and Lachlin down the alley. When they arrived at the tailor's shop, he moved toward the crack of the door. He sniffed deeply, and then let out a grunt.

"This will be more of the same, so be ready," he warned. "Nell, you've never seen anything like this. Maybe you should wait outside."

She shook her head stubbornly. "Nay, I will not."

Peter pushed open the door and they stepped inside.

The smell of metallic fire burned Nell's nostrils. The building was dark, for no candles were lit and all the night shutters had not yet been lifted. Daylight speared the entrance, revealing a lantern overturned on the greeting table.

Peter opened its casing, then lit the wick with a match.

Light blazed into Nell's vision, and she blinked.

That was a mistake.

She would never forget the horror she saw next.

Scattered on the walls were streaks of stark red blood. Sinewy limbs were strewn all over the room, and Nell had to watch her step, so as not to trip over a severed arm or limbless torso.

As they passed into the main hall, she bit back tears. Flickers of memory flashed in her mind as she pictured her book at home, open to the painting of the *Massacre at Merrill Shrine*. The carnage inside this room was unequalled. Bodies were piled on top of one another, blades still embedded in their cooling flesh.

"There are so few Garshu dead," Lachlin whispered, her voice quivering.

"These people were peaceful tradesmen and farmers," Peter replied quietly. "They knew naught of fighting such beasts. They had no chance."

"The Garshu killed the Giant," Nell noted, feeling ill.

Peter cursed. "Swarming vermin! Even poor Odorff didn't have a hope."

"Half of these people were our conscripts," Nell said bitterly. "They were here to fight with us. Why did we enlist them, if there was no hope?" Her voice raised in volume, along with her frustration. "Why did we even bring them here if there was no chance, Peter?" She shook with fury.

The old man placed his hands on her shoulders.

"Nell, listen to me. We all knew there was only a slim chance that these people would last against the Garshu. They came here because they wanted to, because they believed in us and knew that if we didn't fight the Garshu, we'd all pay the price."

She gazed into his wise eyes, feeling such sorrow that she thought she might burst.

Lachlin gestured to the door. "Come on, let's get out of here and find our friends."

Exiting the building, they discovered Karistaal, Treyton and Liam just rounding the corner. Their expressions were grim, and Liam appeared to be in some sort of daze, as though he could not awake from a bad dream.

"The Garshu must have come in the night," Treyton said unevenly. "It looks like they wiped out everyone at all the inns."

Liam nodded. "They destroyed our entire army in one night, barely losing any of their own. The camps on the outskirts are the same—abandoned, except for those who were slaughtered. It's over."

He crouched down, running a hand through his hair. Despite his best efforts, his mind wandered back to the day he and Lachlin had found their village slaughtered.

"We're back to running," he said in a bleak voice.

The group hesitated in front of the inn, each looking equally defeated.

"I'm going to find Garick," Nell mumbled.

Treyton grabbed her hand. "I'll go with you."

They set off for the inn, the rest of the group following slowly behind, saying nothing. All were too tangled in their own thoughts.

As they approached the inn, Nell realized a peculiar fact.

She paused, a look of confusion on her face.

"If the Garshu were going through Paraan and killing everyone inside the inns, why are *we* still alive? Would they not have wanted us dead most of all?"

"Aye," a voice said from the inn's doorway.

Garick and Bean stepped forward.

"They *did* want to kill us," Garick said. "But we were purposely marked so they would pass us by." He pointed.

Above the inn door was a crimson stripe.

Karistaal's face paled. "Is that—?"

"Blood," Bean concluded. "Garick saw it this morning."

"How could the Garshu have seen that last night?" Peter asked. "It was far too dark."

"They were looking for it," Liam answered. "I'll wager that the Garshu knew one of the inns was going to have that mark, and they just looked carefully before entering."

He pursed his dry lips. "It appears as though the Dwarf, Corin, was right. Someone has betrayed us. They've given our plans to the Garshu, and for some reason, arranged to have our lives spared." He paused. "The odd thing is, I'm quite surprised a Garshulan would agree to spare us under any circumstance."

A grumble of agreement trickled through the group.

Nell peered at the bloodstain above the door.

Liam was right. Someone had deceived them, and yet safeguarded them.

The question, however, is who...and why?

Chapter Twenty

The screams of the citizens of Paraan filled the air like never before. Discovering their loved ones brutally slaughtered was more than they could bear. Many of the Garshu's victims had been visitors, but quite a few were much loved Paraanians who had been working at the inns.

Nell sat on the bed in her room, her chin on her palms while her fingers pulled absentmindedly at her earlobes. She stared out the window, watching people struggle to drag what was left of their loved ones from the various inns.

She had suggested that they volunteer to assist the townsfolk, but everyone else thought that it would be a bad idea. Too many emotions were flaring, and they did not need to draw any more anger by pushing their presence.

Disheartened, she had informed Treyton that she wanted to be alone. She had come upstairs, cried, and now was sitting in a stupor of contemplation and hopelessness, as she watched the morbid tasks through her window.

Thoughts ran through her mind at an alarming rate.

How could these creatures kill so many innocent people? Why did someone decide to spare us? Who did it? How did they know what we were doing and where? How can we possibly defeat the Garshu now?

This last thought surprised Nell, and she drew her eyes from the streets to gaze upon her sword. It stood propped up against the wall, the hilt gleaming in the sunlight that streamed through the window.

"There must be something we can do," she murmured.

From the corner of her eye, a movement diverted her attention. She swiftly reached for the sword, drawing it out of its sleeve in a matter of seconds.

Then she faced the intruder.

A wee toddler sat upright on the floor by the door. He was looking down at something in his hands.

Nell neared him, confused.

The child looked up, stopping her in her tracks. Her own mint-green eyes stared back as the child gnawed on the toy in his hand—the wooden doll Garick had given her—the one he said her father had made.

The sword fell from her hands, clanking onto the bedroom floor. Just as she reached for the toddler, hands grasped the child, lifting him into the air.

"No, Coada, don't eat that."

The voice echoed inside Nell's head, and she placed a hand to her temple. She watched as the hands around Coada evolved into arms, a torso, legs and a head. A long, black mane framed a face she knew well. She would know Treyton's smile anywhere, though she had never seen him as happy as he was now, when he hugged the child.

She reached out for them, but seized only air, the vision evaporating in a flash. She felt a terrible loss like never before and she longed for the vision to return.

A plan began to form in her mind. Before long, she was packing her bags, determination on her face and in her heart. As she descended the stairs, she noticed the tranquillity that engulfed the inn. When she reached the main floor, she was stunned.

There was not a soul in sight.

The dining hall was empty, its doors pulled shut. The common room on her left was vacant as well. Sounds of grief crept inside from an open window, its exotically coloured drapes riding the wind. The front door was ajar, sunlight beaming through and lighting the foyer with vibrant serenity in a day full of misery.

She tugged open the door, setting her bags on the front steps. Then she went back upstairs to Treyton's room and knocked.

Liam answered the door.

"What is it?" he asked distractedly, as though he had been sleeping.

His unkempt appearance and inattention made her feel even more confident about her decision to be with Treyton. She would have made a very bad mistake had she followed her premature feelings for Liam.

"Where is Treyton?" she asked.

Liam stepped aside, allowing Treyton to slide past.

Nell saw the lines of stress on his face. She realized that what she was about to tell him would not be accepted easily, if he accepted it at all.

"I must speak with you."

She guided him into the hallway.

"What's wrong?" he asked.

Nell swallowed, took a deep breath and released it. She looked into Treyton's eyes and a memory of her vision—of their little boy—flashed in her mind.

"I am going to do something," she said. "I need to ask you to trust me and stay here where you are safe. I hope whoever painted that doorframe still means us well."

Confused, Treyton raised a hand and caressed her arm.

"Nell, I don't understand."

She shook her head, frowning. "Treyton, right now you cannot understand. And I do not think I want you to. I do not think you would allow me to go if you knew what my intentions were. That is why you must trust me."

Treyton gripped her arm, as though that would keep her firmly planted in front of him. She sighed, taking his hand in hers.

"I have seen something," she whispered. "I have had

my first vision. The sight would have stopped your heart, for it contained so much joy and promise. That is why I must go." She pulled away from his grip.

"But why?"

Sunlight from the window at the end of hall sprayed radiance on his hair. The very form of him—so strapping and fervent—pulled at her heart. She drank in the moment.

"Because I need to make sure that vision comes true."

She stared at him, strengthened by her decision.

Treyton paused, gave a barely visible nod, and then returned to his room. He turned in the doorway, his eyes trailing after her as she walked toward the room she shared with Lachlin.

Once his door clicked shut, Nell sprinted downstairs.

Outside, the heat of the day struck her. She lifted her bags onto her shoulders, making sure she was still able to withdraw her sword.

Then she began her journey out of Paraan.

Passing various townsfolk, she lowered her eyes. Most of them did not see her, but those who did certainly voiced their judgments. She was quite ashamed by the time she passed through the borders of Paraan. She was relieved to be free of their jeers, but a sense of foreboding swept through her. This was the first time she had ever been anywhere on her own.

Her thoughts strayed to Garick. She was overwhelmed by the feeling of loss that was associated with every thought of him.

"Be of cheer, Nell!" she muttered. "You are doing a great thing today. Think not of the pain, but dwell on a pleasant memory instead."

She forced a smile, recalling a memory of when she was a little girl. One day, Garick had asked her to pick herbs from their garden. She had been stung by a stingsect and she had raced to him in tears. He picked her up after she showed him her throbbing hand, the green stinger still embedded in her skin.

He had carefully pulled it out, wiped her tears from

her eyes and kissed her hand. Magically, he pulled a lavender flower from behind his back and presented it to her. She forgot all about her hand as she grasped the flower. She kissed Garick on the cheek and leapt down from his arms. Hugging his knees, she then skipped off to play.

Nell sighed.

The memory, once fond, was now bittersweet and painful. Wrapped up in her thoughts, she almost failed to notice a faint clanging behind her.

Someone was following her.

Whoever it was, he stayed a safe distance behind, but he was hot on her trail, nonetheless. Tracking her.

Night began to slowly unveil.

She passed through Cholart and stopped on its southern border. Unpacking her dinner, she gazed at the stars and thought of the night she and Lachlin had spent talking under the stars outside of Pandrag. She was certain that Lachlin had some ill feeling toward her, but she was unsure why.

As Nell thoughtfully chewed on a roll, a muffled noise behind her caught her attention. In a heartbeat, she withdrew her sword and faced the direction from which the noise had come.

The bushes shuddered.

"Whoever you are, show yourself," she commanded. "Do not believe I would hesitate to run you through."

Despite the quiver in her voice, she sounded brave.

The bushes shook once more.

Then someone spoke from within. "Please, don't strike me. I was waiting for you to fall asleep, so I could steal some of your food. I've been travelling for many days and I'm starving." A figure emerged from the foliage. "Please."

A hungry-looking Elf stood before, his hood lowered.

She stared into his eyes.

"Have we met before?" she asked.

"Dintik," the Elf answered. "My name is Dintik."

She lowered her sword. "Yes, I remember you from

the registration. What are you doing out here?"

Dintik hesitated. "In truth, I followed you. I saw you leave without any of your kin. I wanted to leave too, but I did not want to be alone after barely escaping last night's massacre. I thought maybe I'd be able to follow you without you noticing, but it seems I failed." He stood by the bushes looking very vulnerable.

She sheathed her blade and gestured him forward.

"If you are so famished, Elf, come eat. I do not have much, but you are welcome to share."

Dintik's eyes flickered. They cleared, as though a fog had been plaguing them.

"I lied to you," he admitted. "I have food. I was just curious about you. Pardon my prying. I-I'm sorry." He backed away, his movements jerky.

Before she could say a word, the Elf was gone.

She frowned, feeling strangely bereft after Dintik's abrupt departure. She could not explain it, but for some reason she felt attached to him. Shrugging it off as mere whimsy, she sat back down to enjoy her meal. Her sword stayed close beside her.

Dintik fled back to his cart. He had hidden it behind a cluster of trees. He skidded in behind it and threw back the tarp that covered one side. He pulled out a box, setting it upon his lap. Then he removed a long dagger from his belt.

Opening the lid of the box, he dropped the dagger inside, as though it were filthy. He shuddered, and then thrust the box back into the cart. He sat there for a moment, contemplating what he had planned to do…and how he could not follow through.

It had been *her*. There was no doubt. But how could he do it? She had the answers for which he had been searching all these years.

The forest surrounded him in shades of green and gold, while the wildlife kept their distance. Yet amidst the beauty of the woodland, Dintik could only fight back tears and wish his life had turned out differently.

"Gone?" Garick asked in disbelief. "No, she cannot be."

Everyone stood in the room that Lachlin and Nell had shared.

"Her belongings are all gone," Lachlin said. "And there are villagers who saw her leave. They suggested that we follow her." She ran a hand through her hair, feeling the stress of the moment. "The citizens want us out of Paraan. I say we go, before one of them decides to gut us in our sleep. There are many angry people here, and although we didn't wield the blades in these deaths, we still caused them."

"But where could Nell have gone?" Karistaal asked.

Treyton's face was lined with deep worry. "All she said to me was that she had her first vision and she needed to make sure it was going to come true. She told me she was planning on going somewhere, that I wouldn't let her go if she told me where." He wrung his hands.

There was an awkward silence in the room.

"The lot of you can stay here for all I care," Garick said finally. "But she is my ward, so I am following her." He turned to Lachlin. "You say there were townsfolk who saw her leave. Which direction did she take?"

"The woman I spoke with saw her take the south road. Toward Cholart."

"Then that is the road I take. She is only a few hours ahead. She will probably stop for camp once it darkens, but I will not. I will reach her before morning."

"You mean *we* will," Treyton added, giving Garick a look that said there was no sense arguing.

"Aye," Peter added. "We stay together. Family."

Chapter Twenty-One

The townsfolk glared and spat at them as they departed Paraan. It was sad to see that those who had heralded their presence only a day before now resented them.

Garick kicked dust at many who called out. He did not shy at returning their unkind words.

"Go on back to work, you lazy bunch!" he yelled.

An air of depression hovered over them as they reached the borders. The sun had set, casting an orange glow upon their sombre faces.

Peter rode between them. "Let me tell you a tale—the fable of the great wise-woman Nanauline." He cleared his throat. *"With beauty enough to stop men's hearts, and wisdom to earn respect from the Goddess, Nanauline set forth across Cantro, in search of a way to make her name live forever..."*

The band hiked toward Cholart, each visualizing the story as it unfolded. Soon, night fell.

A thin, cold hand covered Nell's mouth, abruptly rousing her from sleep. Panicking, she reached for her blade, only to discover it was held by the person muffling her. She swiped at the hand on her face, and then spun around.

A mute signal silenced her.

The hood of the cloak fell back, revealing Dintik. He had a look of dire concern upon his face as he gestured for her to follow him in the direction of a leafy clump of trees about forty paces to her left.

Unsure of his intentions, she followed the gaunt looking Elf, alert and on guard. When he leaned toward her, she jerked back. He held his hands up in peace.

A moment later, he beckoned her near.

She readied her blade.

"About fifty paces further," he whispered. "On our right. Look carefully."

She peered between two Thistonberry bushes. Her heart stopped when she saw the distinctive metal boots on two bodies lying beside a dying campfire. Upon careful inspection, she could make out at least two more sleeping figures.

Dintik motioned for them to head back. She nodded, this time wholeheartedly following him. They reached camp and she noticed that the Elf had already moved his cart. It sat close to where she had been sleeping.

"Their disgusting cooking woke me," Dintik said in a low voice. "I waited until they were sleeping to move away. It was pure luck that they didn't decide to camp further along, or else they would have discovered us both."

Nell hastily packed her bedroll.

"I need to go, before they wake," she whispered. "Thank you for warning me. You have proven you do not bear me ill will, so you are welcome to—"

She broke off when the Elf suddenly yanked his hood over his head and cowered behind her.

"What is it?" she hissed.

She gripped her blade and spun around.

"Watch where you swing that, girl," Garick scolded.

Her heart returned to a steady pace at the sight of her guardian. Behind him, the others rushed forward.

Treyton grabbed her, pulling her into a suffocating hug.

"Why would you leave without me?" he demanded. "Without us? What were you thinking?"

"Shh!" she commanded. "Keep your voices low. There are enemies afoot. Let me collect my things. We must leave immediately."

Gathering her few belongings, she led them away, irritated by their presence. She yearned to go on alone. They would never aid her in her plan. How could she tell them to leave?

What am I going to do?

When they were far enough away from danger, she turned to them. "There was a small group of Garshu asleep not far from where you found me."

Garick stiffened, and then cast a look toward the bushes.

Nell pursed her lips. "Say, where is the Elf? Did he not follow us?" When no one replied, she said, "An Elf followed me from Paraan. He woke me when he discovered the Garshu."

However, Dintik and his cart were gone.

"Oh well, I suppose he is better off on his own anyway." She paused. "I cannot tell you where I am going, nor can I ask you to aid me. You must let me go. *Alone.*"

She stared beseechingly at Treyton.

"Absolutely not," he said, shaking his head.

"Out of the question," Garick reinforced. "You are going home."

He grabbed her arm and she dropped the sword.

"Garick!" she cried, her voice echoing through the woods.

She cringed, then snatched her arm away, picked up her sword and straightened her tunic.

"You will listen to me, for once," she said, gritting her teeth. "Now, before those Garshu come barging over here, you had better shush and follow me."

She stormed off toward Sorcha Forest.

Hours passed, and they entered the forest just as the sun began to peek over the land.

Nell set down her pack, slumped next to a tree and opened her water flask.

Everyone ogled at her, impatient for an explanation.

Karistaal let out a sigh. "Nell, my dear, tell us what this is all about." She leaned against Peter, the pair looking weary.

Nell felt a surge of guilt.

She swallowed hard. "I-I had my first vision. It was…amazing." A lump formed in her throat at the very thought of it. "All hope of waging a war against the Garshu is lost. Somehow, they knew what we were doing, and yet they spared us. They are playing with us. A show of power."

"We will find others to aid us," Garick insisted.

Nell shook her head. "We cannot give rusty swords to farmers and hope to wipe out an entire race of Garshu. We all know how quickly they reproduce. The only way to fight them is to go after the Garshulas."

"Aye, Nell, we know this," Liam said wearily. "That's what we were going to do, remember? March in with our own army and destroy them. But you've said so yourself—all hope is lost." He released an exhausted breath. "Let's go back to hiding from the Garshu. We can go home with you and Garick until we figure out where to go next. No more planning and then having those plans fail. So many have needlessly died because of us. Let it go."

"Go then," she said, lifting her chin. "You can do whatever you want, Liam. However, I will not go home. I intend to continue. The Garshu must die. They must pay for what they have done. No one will stand up to them and they will swarm Cantro soon enough. No one— *nothing*—will be left."

She sighed. "I am heading to the nests alone. I will sneak in and kill the Garshulas. If the other reproduces before I get to her, I will kill the egg as well."

Everyone stared at her as though she were mad.

Then Peter smiled. "You, my girl, are too much. Do you really believe you could get in alone? You'll need at least a few of us to help. The nests will be heavily guarded."

"We need a diversion," Treyton murmured. "One that will draw the Garshu away from the nests. Who has the map?"

Bean's shaky hands pulled out the worn parchment. He handed it to Treyton, who gripped the boy's shoulder and gave him a reassuring look.

Treyton flattened out the map. "If we can somehow get the Garshu to head north, we could shortcut past Fairsome and get there unseen."

"What could we possibly do to get them to move?" Liam asked. "There are masses of Garshu already in Santz, running those pits."

Bean released an uneasy laugh. "Maybe this ain't a good idea. I mean, how could we get to the caves, sneak into the nests and murder the Garshula? We're too few. The idea is crazy!"

"Fine," Garick said begrudgingly. "We will go to the caves. We do need to go with Treyton's idea, though. We need a diversion. It is not as if we have a mighty army to go marching in with. We cannot just scare them off."

Lachlin stared at the map with fearful fascination.

"Is this where we are?" She pointed to Sorcha Forest.

"Aye," Liam answered.

He studied the map with her for a moment, then motioned Peter and Treyton aside. While they were speaking, Karistaal and Nell broke away, and Bean stared into the distance.

Lachlin traced a finger over the map until she reached the caves. Her finger swept over the land and onto three words.

Three Daggers Sea.

A wave of icy fear ran through her and she yanked her hand away.

It's inevitable.

She gazed at her family.

Good-hearted, stoic Liam. Karistaal—the only mother she had really known. Peter. Who could ask for a more loving father figure? Bean was like a little brother, yet so strong. And Treyton? The only man she had ever loved. The only man she ever would love.

But he loves Nell.

"I know a way." She spoke barely above a whisper. When no one responded, she raised her voice. "I know how to divert them!"

Immediate silence greeted her.

"What's your idea, sister?" Liam asked, puzzled.

Lachlin took a deep breath.

They would never believe her if she told the truth.

"We'll travel to Hourling together," she said. "Then I'll leave to make contact with some...*folk* I know. They'll help us, but only right after I ask them. We must attack the Garshu immediately after."

"What folk are these?" Treyton demanded. "Why did you not tell us you had contacts there before?"

"I can't explain. Once you reach—" Lachlin consulted the map once more, "*here*, stop and wait for me. It's imperative that I go alone. I'll meet you at this beach when I'm through."

"I can't believe we're going to do this," Bean mumbled.

Nell moved away, lost in thought.

"Nell," Lachlin called. "I must speak with you before we go."

The two women took privacy behind a cluster of bushes.

Lachlin removed her gloves.

"I'd like to see your vision," she explained. "It has given you enough reason to try to take on the Garshu by yourself, and I need that conviction to complete my quest. Please."

She held out her hands.

Nell nodded, silent.

"Thank you," Lachlin said. "Now close your eyes and take yourself back to where you were when it began.

Don't remember it; just think of where you were before it
happened. When I touch you, it'll begin again." She
smiled grimly. "Seeing another's visions is the only time I
see one normally, instead of living it as I usually do."

Nell closed her eyes and pictured the room at the inn.
She soon felt Lachlin's warm hands wrap around hers,
and it immediately was as if fire were passing through her
veins.

She opened her eyes in alarm, only to find that she
was sitting beside the window at the inn. Lachlin was on
the bed.

Nell flicked an eager look over her shoulder.

She was not disappointed.

There he is!

With the emerald eyes of her family and Treyton's dark
hair, her son played with the doll. Treyton's joyful face
soon came into view, and she watched him pick up the
boy. When they disappeared, she experienced the same
stabbing loss.

She looked at Lachlin and blinked.

Nell was back in the forest, standing across from
Lachlin, their hands separated. They stared at each other,
eyes wide and damp with salty tears.

Lachlin took a shaky step back, tugging on her gloves.

"Are you all right?" Nell asked.

Lachlin held up a hand. "I'm fine."

They stood in silence for a moment.

"Was he not beautiful?" Nell whispered finally.

Lachlin folded her arms across her chest and stared at
the ground. After a moment, she lifted her head, her
tearful eyes meeting Nell's as she smiled through her
pain.

"Truly worth it."

Chapter Twenty-Two

Lachlin pensively moved toward the shoreline. Her heart was beating so hard in her chest that she was sure someone would hear it. Unfortunately, there was no one nearby.

She had shed most of her garments—including her gloves and scarf—so that all she wore was a beige slip. The sheer fabric danced seductively in the sea air.

She removed her shoes before stepping onto the beach. Her toes sank into the moist sand, as though they were disappearing into cake batter. Each step brought her closer to the place she had spent her entire life avoiding.

At the water's edge, she wrapped her arms around her body. Then she raised a tentative hand to her neck. She was not surprised to feel that the scar had swelled—even worse than when she had her nightmares.

The water ebbed and advanced, nipping at her toes. She watched it, then closed her eyes and tried to calm her breathing.

In…out. In…

Composed, she released a long breath and opened her eyes. The sun was setting, and as she watched it, she swallowed hard.

My last sunset.

A ripple of water inched closer, the first icy touch on

her toes. Then it was gone. Soon enough, it was back, this time washing up to her ankles.

They were coming.

A wave splashed her legs, while a distant rumbling echoed in the air. She gasped as the sky quickly darkened and the sound grew louder.

The scar around her neck began to burn.

A creature rose out of the water, its skin translucent—sickly—and its ash-grey hair looking like it had survived some great fire.

Although it had been ten cycles, Lachlin recognized her.

Balancing on an enormous fin, the Mermaid stood to her full height. She had to have been easily nine feet tall. She seemed to quiver, as if her physical self had caused the waves.

"You have been evading us, Human," she said abrasively.

Lachlin shivered. "I've come to make another bargain with you." She was surprised at the strength in her voice.

"No, you will come now. We need your spirit. It has been many moons since a Human spirit was fed to us."

The burning scar on Lachlin's neck pulsated and she winced at the pain. When the Mermaid beckoned, the sea pulled her further into its deathly grip.

"I can offer you more!" she cried out, desperate. "You can finally have me, but you can also have so many more. Thousands! Their spirits would be yours forever."

The Mermaid's eyes narrowed and her lips curved into a sly smirk. "How, Human? Tell me how."

"There is a battle about to be waged not far from here," Lachlin said. "If we were to drive these enemies onto the beach, would you take them?"

The Mermaid laughed. "Why do you ask questions to which you already know the answers? You know we cannot grasp what has not felt us first."

The sand shifted beneath Lachlin's feet, bringing her closer to the Mermaid.

"Wait!" Lachlin pleaded. "I will draw them into the

water, but you must let me go now. I need to help my kin get these enemies here."

The Mermaid's face darkened. "You cannot be set free. You have promised your spirit to us. Saros knows that promises cannot be broken."

Icy water enveloped Lachlin up to her waist.

"Please!" she cried. "Let me notify my kin of this new bargain and I *will* come back to you. I swear it! I'll bring you thousands of spirits."

The very sand beneath her feet trembled, and the scent of all the seas she would never know wafted in the air. Salty seawater crawled up her chest, then upward still, until it cooled the burning on her neck. The water rendered her helpless.

"Wait!" she sputtered in panic.

The Mermaid swam closer in one fluid movement and paused an arm's length away. "You know in your spirit what our terms will be, Human."

Lachlin nodded eagerly. "I'll have them step into the water near the caves. I only have one thing to ask of you."

"What makes you think you are in any position to ask for anything?" the Mermaid quipped.

"Please," she said, straining to keep her head above the surface. "Once the spirits enter your waters, they'll try to do me harm. I need you to protect me until they all enter the sea. It must be this way. *All* of them."

The sea rose to Lachlin's chin. Salt water entered her mouth and she spat it out, her eyes frantically awaiting an answer.

"Agreed," the Mermaid said after a long moment. "We will acquire them. And then we will acquire you."

Lachlin found herself standing on the beach, facing the sea, her skin and hair as dry as the sand she stood upon.

A frothy wave curled in at her, spitefully teasing her.

She spun on one heel and ran.

"Where is she?" Liam muttered, pacing between two

trees near the beach.

They were resting in a small clearing that was bordered by a few scraggly trees and bushes. The sun had just finished setting and the night was beginning to cool.

Liam stared at the stars and reflected on their trip to the small village of Hourling. It had been more exciting than they would have liked. Armies of Garshu had scoured the lands as they passed through, and Liam could take a good guess at who the creatures were looking for.

Unfortunately, that was not the only misfortune to have greeted them.

While hunting for food, Peter had tripped among some rocks, spraining his right ankle. As if things were not bad enough, the moment they arrived in Hourling, Bean disappeared again.

Liam glanced at Nell. "Why would Bean leave?"

"Maybe he is afraid?" she suggested. "He did seem apprehensive about this idea."

"He'll be back," Karistaal murmured, staring off into the distance.

Peter lovingly rubbed her back while he sat on a fallen tree, his foot splinted and wrapped in rags.

Treyton moved behind Nell, enveloping her in his arms. They had gone public with their affections, and Garick was the only one bothered by their relationship.

When the Elf witnessed their embrace, he walked away.

Liam turned his attention back to his vigil.

Where are you, Lachlin?

There were so many questions left unanswered when Lachlin left. She refused to tell anyone where she was going—or why. What if she had been hurt? How would he find her? How long before they should go looking for her? These questions constantly trickled through his mind until he could think of nothing else. Not even the impending battle.

He glanced at the others.

Treyton was engrossed in watching Nell's every move.

His thoughts were not of the upcoming battle either. He was thinking that he would not let Nell slip away from him again.

Karistaal and Peter tended to each other, like always, but their eyes remained focused on the distance. Karistaal searched for signs of Lachlin or Bean, and Peter watched for Garshu.

Garick, who paced nearly as much as Liam did, was thinking only of the Garshu. He still chastised himself for not attacking the ones who had slept in the woods near Follok. As they had travelled toward Hourling, there were other opportunities to run into Garshu, but they had evaded them. Shedding Garshu blood was nearly all Garick could think of. *That* and the fact that Treyton and Nell were a little too close for comfort.

Liam's gaze shifted to Nell. "What are you thinking?"

Nell was worried. It struck her as ironic that she was most concerned about Lachlin, especially since they had not really hit it off as friends.

"It is too dark," she said. "Will we even see her?"

He pondered this for a moment.

"Let's just make sure we're all watching and listening," he said. "It's possible she could walk right past us unnoticed."

He seemed bothered by this thought, and Nell almost felt bad for bringing it up.

"There!" Karistaal shouted, waving.

A figure on horseback approached them.

"What took you so long?" Liam demanded as Lachlin reigned in her horse and jumped to the ground.

Wordlessly, his sister hugged him, and he was taken aback by the show of affection.

"I'm sorry, brother," she said, smiling grimly. "But our hope is restored. We must march immediately, for they'll be waiting for us."

"No more games, love," Peter said in a firm voice. "Tell us, who are you speaking of?"

Everyone studied Lachlin curiously, but she shook her head. "We haven't time now. We must get to the caves."

"And what would you have us do with our army of eight—*seven* now that Bean has gone again?" Treyton asked with fire in his eyes. "Walk in and demand peace? How about we just give up our blades and surrender the last of our kind to them?"

He placed a loving hand on Nell's back, and Lachlin felt a stabbing in her heart at the sight.

"Please," she said. "This is our only chance." She leapt onto her horse and grasped the reigns. "Either you accompany me, or I'll have to do this all on my own."

Without hesitation, Nell mounted her horse. Her friends reluctantly followed suit, and they rode briskly, the horses not given a moment's rest.

Peter pulled up beside Lachlin, forcing her to slow.

"Tell me!" His voice was a whisper, but for the conviction behind it, it could have been a bellow.

She looked at him, and then gazed toward the jagged ridge of rock that held the caves.

And the Garshulas.

Her eyes swept back to Peter. She raised a hand to her throat and slid down the scarf, just enough to show him the reddened wound that now gaped, reopened on her neck.

Peter nearly reigned in his horse at the sight. He stared at her, trying to comprehend.

"No more questions," Lachlin said. "It's my destiny."

They continued on, with Lachlin and Nell leading the way. At the beach close to the caves, they drew to a stop and dismounted, securing their horses in the camouflage of dense bushes.

"What do we do, sister?" Liam asked, his voice giving away his fear. "You've led us to what? Our death?"

"No, Liam," she said, laying a comforting arm on his. "I have led us to hope. Nell had a brilliant idea all along, but we lost sight of it somehow. Going in with an army was the wrong approach. Going in secretly was the right idea. Destroy the Garshulas, and *then* raise our armies. What hope will they have when they realize they can never reproduce? Wiping them out then will be all too easy."

She faced them all. "We need Liam and Garick to take one cave. Nell and Treyton will take the other. Peter and Kris will be the watch. And I—" Lachlin took a deep breath. "I will be the bait."

A murmur of shock swept over them.

"Bait?" Liam demanded. "No, I won't agree to—"

"We do not have a choice," Nell interrupted. "What is your plan, Lachlin?"

"First, we'll lead them out to the beach. Let them see only me, by the water. That will draw them away from the entrances. You can eliminate those in the caves. And Garick will take out any that come along by surprise."

"What about the Dukev?" Nell asked.

"We'll deal with them when—or *if*—we meet them," Liam said.

Nell gave a nod, and then frowned. "It was really a poor time for Bean to go off again. We could have used his blade."

"Why don't *I* go as bait?" Karistaal suggested. "Lachlin is a stronger fighter than I."

"No!" Lachlin cried. "I will be the bait. I don't want any one of you stepping anywhere near the water. Do you understand?"

They all nodded, remaining silent and thoughtful.

Nell broke the calm. "When should we begin?"

"Now," Garick urged, his hand on his bow and his eyes full of deadly lust. "Let us go now."

Lachlin looked skyward. "Aye. Now is the time."

An air of solemnity gripped them as they prepared.

Liam swiftly laced the air with his sword, warming his limbs. Then he hesitantly moved towards his sister. He was not used to feeling such awkwardness around her, but Lachlin had taken a leadership role so suddenly that it was strange for him.

He stood behind her as she stared out to sea.

"Lach—"

"Please, brother," she begged, without turning. "Go with my love." There was an eerie calm in her voice.

Before he could respond, Lachlin strode toward the caves…and the beach. She knew that soon enough the Garshu would see her and they would attack. Sword in hand, she dragged it lifelessly at her side. The sharp tip sliced a line in the sand, marking her undulating path.

Liam watched her leave, and a piece of him left with her. Something in the pit of his stomach told him not to let her go, that she might not return. Deep down, he knew they had no other choice.

Lachlin…

A few paces away, Karistaal readied the horses for the short journey to the mouth of the caves. Nell walked past, certain that she recognized Karistaal's whispered words—an Achocran prayer.

Treyton strode toward her. "We should go, Nell."

"I know."

She watched Lachlin dissipate into the night, disliking the woman being used as bait. Lachlin was such a useful fighter, and Nell did not understand why she refused Karistaal's offer. Or why she was so determined that no one go near the water.

"Come," Treyton urged.

Nell's gaze rested on him, her eyes reflecting his determination and fear.

"Yes, my love. Let us end this."

Chapter Twenty-Three

The caves were enormous, forbidding. The jagged openings sat side-by-side and loomed over the group, further darkening their way as though something had eclipsed the rising moons.

Leaving Karistaal and Peter behind to watch for trouble, Nell, Treyton, Garick and Liam were rooted in what seemed to be a foreign jungle. Tall, wiry trees enveloped them. Prickly bushes and indigo-coloured grass swelled between every crevice.

Nell and Treyton took the cave to the right, and Liam and Garick headed left.

Something was wrong.

Nell could not help but feel that it was rather strange that they had not encountered any Garshu up to this point. Or the Dukev.

They should be guarding the entrances.

Her skin prickled and she stopped dead in her tracks.

Treyton laid a hand on her lower back, but for the first time she found no comfort in his touch.

"What?" he whispered.

She shook her head. Then she gazed before her, seeing only unending darkness.

"What is it, Nell?"

Her blood ran ice cold. "I do not know."

It was not until Treyton lightly nudged her that she

remembered she could walk. She crept forward, cautious and aware. As they continued, she felt worse—as if the air lacked oxygen.

The fading light from outside dimmed quickly.

Nell reached in her pocket, extracting her matches. Treyton already had the torch out and ready. Once lit, the torch flared, filling the entrance with a fiery glow.

The cave ceiling tapered lower as they advanced and the walls curled in a circular motion, leading them left. They followed the path until they reached a corner where the cave ended.

Nell was stunned. "Where do we—"

"There!" Treyton whispered, pointing to a small opening.

Nell realized they must not be using the same entrance the Garshu did, for they would never have fit through an opening so narrow. Comforted, she began to relax and focused her energies on the sword in her hand and the trail before her.

They slid through the opening sideways. It led into a tiny square chamber, lit by a single torch mounted to the wall in the opposite corner. A powder had changed the colour of the walls from a muddy black to sandy beige. The room was empty, except for the torch and a pedestal that stood near a wooden door.

Nell strode to the pedestal.

A large tome rested on it, open to a half-written page. A large leather strip lay down its centre, marking it.

"What is it?" Treyton whispered.

"It is in their language," she said quietly. "This looks to be some sort of record. There is no dust, so someone must be in here at least daily." She flipped through some of the pages, reading bits and pieces. "It is their history— their version of it, anyways." She turned back to the spot where she had found it open.

"Only one way to go," Treyton said grimly, clenching his jaw.

They inched toward the door.

Treyton reached for the wooden latch. Lifting it

carefully, he pulled the earthen door open a crack and gasped at what lay within.

Nell nudged him forward.

The room before them was lit by numerous torches. Circular in design, it was lined with several doors on one side. On the other side, however, was a sight Nell could never have imagined.

A Garshula sat asleep on the earthen floor. She was the size of at least four Giants, rolled into one globular whitish-grey mass. Layers of opalescent fat rested one atop another, until they finally merged at the neck where a bubble-shaped, oval face slumped.

Her eyes were closed. Its mouth was distinctively Garshu, with crimson lips like freshly torn flesh. Drool hung suspended from her lower lip.

The Garshula groaned.

Nell froze.

They were out in the open, exposed, swords raised.

The creature shifted to one side, her flesh flowing like sheer fabric and quivering like water, although her eyes remained closed. Then she groaned again and settled.

Nell carefully sidestepped to the right.

A pile of rocks was stacked behind the Garshula, and as Nell neared them, she saw a slimy, purplish-black rock next to an outstretched appendage. The Garshula's hand.

Nell recoiled in fear, a look of repulsion on her face.

"Those are her *eggs*," she hissed.

Treyton was about to reassure her, but a familiar voice came from the shadows behind the sleeping monstrosity.

"Fascinating, is it not?"

Bean emerged, a smile on his face.

"What are you doing here, Bean?" Nell whispered, relieved. "How did you get in? Are you all right?"

She lowered her sword and began to walk toward him, but Treyton yanked her back.

She flashed him a look of confusion. "What?"

Treyton's face darkened and he shook his head.

She eyed Bean. He did not look like the quiet boy Nell knew. He possessed a strange look and a rakish grin.

"It's really quite interesting," he said in a loud voice. "A Garshula can sleep for long lengths of time, and not much can wake her—not even our voices. They awake when they are ready." He laid a loving hand on the Garshula's gelatinous skin. "Yet, even in her inactivity, she can still reproduce at a startling rate."

Shock surged through Nell's body.

Then came understanding.

She studied Bean with new eyes—the same eyes she looked at the Garshu with. The same ones she had looked at Garick with that night in Paraan. Eyes full of distrust and distaste.

"You have betrayed us, Bean." The hurt was evident in Treyton's voice. "You were the one who told the Garshu of the rebellion. *You* had the soldiers murdered."

"Soldiers!" Bean scoffed. "You call those pathetic farmers, *soldiers*? They would have marched in here and been slaughtered by the Garshu's laughter. I did you a favour by wiping them out. Then you did just as I knew you would. You came here on your own, led by your almighty leader—your sign from Saros." He spat the last words as he glared at Nell.

She realized something then. The boy's high-pitched voice came across well spoken and hinted at an accent that she had never noticed before—Garshurian.

"Where are the Garshu?" she asked, her calm voice masking the fear she felt.

Bean smirked. "They are everywhere! They saw you enter—they're all outside waiting. They've been told not to touch you until I give the word."

Treyton stepped forward, his face twisted in anger. "So you marked the inn in Paraan, only to have us come here and be killed? Deceiver!" He lunged at Bean.

His sword was met instantly by another, and the two pressed against one another—blade of man and blade of boy.

They stood face-to-face, neither moving.

"I don't wish to fight you, Treyton," Bean said. "Though I will if I must. I suggest you drop your sword.

Let me continue with what I was saying."

Nell's mind was numb. Nothing made sense.

"Let him speak," she said.

The former friends broke apart and stepped away, each alert to the other's intent.

Treyton glared at Bean. "You were like a brother to me. How could you do this?"

Nell tugged on his sleeve. "The others are in danger."

"No, they aren't," Bean said. "By now, they are dead."

She sucked in a breath as a sharp vision of her friends flashed through her mind.

"What do you mean?" Her voice quivered.

"The Garshu were told not to touch you. But I told them they could have their way with the others."

Nell closed her eyes and quieted her breathing.

Garick, Karistaal, Peter, Liam, Lachlin...

She could still sense them.

Her eyes flashed open and she watched Bean from beneath her eyelashes.

"There is doubt in your eyes, Bean."

The boy's face became stone and he shrunk a little at her confidence.

She stalked toward him. "Do you know why we are here? Did you figure that out too?"

Bean backed away.

"We are here to kill the Garshulas as you knew, but how will we? There are only a few of us. How can we do it? Tell me, Bean!"

She shoved him, and he stumbled back, barely keeping his balance.

"Do not touch me! Allagh! Shoyg!"

But no one came to help him.

Terror crept into his eyes. "Allagh! *Come now!* Shoyg!"

She shoved him again. Harder.

Bean's arms flailed and he fell to the ground, nearly landing on the pile of eggs. Treyton stomped a foot on the boy's chest, pinning him down, while his sword pressed against Bean' throat.

Nell bent over the boy, her eyes hard. "Do you know

why they are not coming?"

Bean struggled, then slumped back, defeated. "Why?"

Nell smiled. "Because you are all alone here."

"Garick?"

Liam held his torch aloft. He had somehow lost the Elf when they had entered a maze of tunnels. When he heard no reply, he continued on, his heart beating like thunder in his ears.

There was a door ahead.

He looked over his shoulder at the empty passageway. *Not a wretched soul in sight.*

He lifted the latch on the door. He could barely see inside, for blocking his view was the backside of the most hideous creature he had ever seen. It was enormous and took up at least a third of the chamber.

He glanced at the floor.

Between him and the Garshula was a pile of—

"Eggs!" he whispered.

Horrified, he stared at them. Taking a breath, he slipped through the door, sword drawn.

Something moved across the room.

Garick!

Liam saw recognition in his friend's eyes as he skirted the sleeping Garshula and moved cautiously toward Garick.

"We lost each other, eh, friend?" Liam whispered.

"Have you seen a Garshulan?" Garick asked.

"No."

"Whatever Lachlin is doing outside is working then."

"Aye, I'm afraid so," Liam said sadly.

Lachlin watched the Garshu approach the waterline. Her stomach muscles clenched and her heart raced.

Breathe.

Her plan had to work.

At first, the Garshu seemed suspicious and fearful.

They stood on the shore and watched her, probably wondering why she was standing in the sea, water up to her waist, with no one around to help her.

With arrogant confidence, the Garshulan closest to the water's edge grinned at her with yellow teeth. Then he barked out an order and the hordes gathering behind him strode into the sea.

Lachlin did not even have to swing her blade. The Mermaid was true to her word. A few steps into the water were all it took. One by one, the waves reached out and swallowed the unsuspecting Garshu.

But not Lachlin. She was protected.

It was a strange feeling to be so powerful, even for a short time. It was fulfilling as well, to find that after so many cycles of fighting and running, she could stand unarmed, while the Garshu fell around her as if they were nothing.

Lachlin ignored their startled roars and wide-eyed terror. They continued to come, mindless in their determination to destroy her. By the time they realized it was a trap, it was already too late.

The Mermaid had her souls.

Lachlin watched blankly. "Soon it will be my turn."

"Do it, Treyton!" Nell screamed. "Now!"

Sword in hand, Treyton stepped toward the Garshula.

"No!" Bean shrieked, knocking Nell aside and jumping to his feet.

Snatching his sword from the ground, the boy leapt at Treyton, the tip of his blade slicing Treyton's shoulder.

Nell scrambled to her feet and kicked her leg out, tripping Bean from behind. The boy crashed into the Garshula.

The creature's eyes flew open.

A profound and agonizing squeal echoed in the room.

When Bean stumbled back, he was covered in a purplish liquid. His blade stood upright, embedded deep in the flesh of the Garshula's body.

Bean's face contorted in horror. "Oh, Saros, No!"

The Garshula moaned and wavered, its body jiggling in pain. The quivering slowly ceased and the creature's eyes drifted shut, lifeless.

Silence.

Bean dropped to his knees, into the fluid that covered the floor. His eyes were full of remorse. "Gras Fiynan Shar." He spoke in perfect Garshurian. "*I'm so sorry.*"

Nell sprinted toward the doorway, fuelled by her astonishment. She was stunned he had spoken Garshurian. Treyton stayed close behind her. She flung open the door and ran for the small crack in the wall. Then they raced through the cave, heading for the moonlight.

"Is your arm all right?" Nell yelled over her shoulder.

"Aye," Treyton called. "It's just a scratch."

They veered toward the second cave.

As they ran, Nell thought of Bean and the Garshula. She could not believe how easy it had been to kill the beast. Only one stab and she was done for.

Most pleasant, Nell found, was the fact that the fearsome Dukev were nothing but a myth—stories carried on to strike fear into the hearts of those who would dare to enter the caves. It was extraordinary that the Garshu had somehow caused the entire nation to believe that the creatures actually existed.

The entrance to the second cave lay ahead and as the path began to wind, she slowed. Treyton ran into her.

"Sorry," he said sheepishly.

She smiled, relit the torch she had shoved into her bag, and then continued forward. She gripped her sword tightly in one hand.

Before long, they passed through a cavernous tunnel, where the ceiling was high. Finally, they came to a door.

As Nell neared it, she heard whispers on the other side.

"Garick?" Treyton asked.

She nodded.

"Are you certain?"

"Absolutely."

The door squeaked open.

Inside, Garick and Liam faced the second sleeping Garshula, swords drawn. Bean stood in front of the creature.

"Took you long enough," he taunted when he saw Nell.

Garick and Liam spun around, their faces relaxing once they saw her.

Treyton followed Nell into the chamber and they joined Garick and Liam. Together, they faced the sleeping Garshula and Bean, who was sweating profusely.

"Somehow you have lured all the Garshu away," the boy whined. "And that annoys me. Since Peter and Karistaal are outside, I can only assume Lachlin is doing something to keep them busy." He grinned at Liam. "Or should I say, they are keeping her busy? I know many a Garshulan who wanted to try out a Human woman." He shrugged. "I guess they'll all just take turns."

Liam charged. "You bastard!"

Within seconds, Bean disarmed Liam and sent his sword skating across the dirt floor. Liam lay at the boy's feet, a bloody wound across his stomach.

Bean raised his sword high above his head.

"No!" Nell cried.

Suddenly, Bean's eyes flared, his face registering shock. The sword slipped through his fingers and clattered to the floor. When he lowered his arms, he saw the arrow piercing his hand. He cried out in anguish and fell back against the wall.

Garick reached for another arrow, ready to nock it.

"Do not move!" he ordered. "Treyton, see to Liam."

Treyton hurried to his friend's side and helped him to his feet.

"My hand," Bean moaned.

He cradled his injured hand to his chest and his eyes watered as he broke the arrow, leaving the shaft lodged in his skin, the tip protruding from his palm.

Then he glared at Nell.

"You cannot win!" he shouted. "The Garshu are greater in number and so much stronger than you feeble Humans."

A memory flashed through Nell's mind, and she smiled at the thought of her son. Without hesitation, she wielded her sword and marched toward the Garshula's progeny.

"No!" Bean screamed, picking up his sword. "I won't let you do it!"

Nell laughed. "With your wounded hand, you cannot fight me. Let it go. I do not understand why you are defending the Garshu anyway."

"It's funny," Bean said to her, "but no one except you noticed the lack of Garshu in Paraan during the recruitment. Did you all really think it would go unnoticed?"

"Perhaps it would have," Treyton spat, "had you not run off and squealed like a pig, you wretched worm."

"Stupid Humans, as if you could deceive the Garshu."

"Bean," Nell said. "You are Human too."

"You have no idea who I am. None of you do." He stared at Nell. "You won't kill me."

"Do not be too sure of that," she replied.

Bean smirked. "I'm the only one who knows where our mother is, *Nelhua*."

Chapter Twenty-four

Nell felt as if a sword had been plunged into her heart. "What are you saying?"

Bean neared her, a cocky look in wide eyes, and for the first time, Nell noticed their mint-green hue.

"I am saying, sister, that our mother is alive. And I know where she is."

Nell whirled around. "Garick, you said you never saw my mother's body. I did not imagine they would have kept her alive."

"It could be true." Liam winced. "Lachlin had a vision of your mother and the day she was taken. But we never thought she was still alive."

"Well, she is!" Bean interjected. "And she gave birth to a wonderful son." He stretched his arms exultantly. "I am the one who is the true heir of Shirell."

She gaped at him in disbelief. "You're lying."

"Don't you understand?" he asked with a laugh. "They kept her alive to show good faith to Saros. When *I* was born, they took me in. They showed me the truth about you Humans, about how you turned the Garshu into slaves."

"But that was Saros' intent," she argued. "That was the Garshu's purpose."

"No, it was not!" the boy snapped. "The Garshu were born to rule. And I, as the soon-to-be last and true heir of

Shirell, will rule them." He confidently raised his sword.

From the corner of her eye, Nell saw Treyton's face. He was terrified for her.

"No, Bean," she said in a quiet voice. "You will not."

She attacked him, her sword catching his, sending it flying through the air. Then she jumped on the boy and pummelled him until he slid to the ground next to the Garshula. Before Bean could regain his senses, she stretched her sword across him and sliced open the belly of the Garshula, releasing a stream of pink fluid.

Bean howled. "No!"

She saw the slimy, white egg behind the dying Garshula, and she drove her sword into it. With a foot on the egg, she extracted the sword and promptly sliced the egg in half. Each piece rolled around like lopsided bowls, the gooey contents spilling over the sides.

"Nell!" Garick roared.

His warning came too late.

Something slammed into her back. She flew through the air, landing hard on the ground.

Bean hovered over her, his face red with anger.

"Seekra!" he bellowed. "You worthless bitch!"

A memory of her recurrent nightmare flashed briefly before her.

She leapt to her feet, grasping her sword with purpose. Blades met and sparks flew wildly, while the two feinted and lunged in an unparalleled display of expert swordsmanship.

Bean stabbed forward. She ran her blade around his in an attempt to disarm him, but he disengaged his sword in one clean movement. When he swung hard at her, she leapt backward, the tip of his blade missing her stomach by a hair's width. For every manoeuvre he tried, she countered, without wounding him.

"I do not wish to hurt you," she cried.

"Too bad, for I will kill you, sister."

"Kill him, Nell!" Garick yelled.

Tears of frustration filled her eyes, blinding her. "No!"

A sharp pain sliced through her arm. Blood trickled

from her right bicep. She stared at him—at her brother.

"She bleeds," he hissed, excited at drawing first blood.

That was the moment Nell realized that there was only one way out. She would have to kill her brother.

She collapsed to her knees, sobbing.

Bean stared at her, confused. "What are you doing? Get up! Fight me!"

She shook her head and laid down her sword.

"I will not kill you," she said, tears streaming down her cheeks. "You are my brother. Come with me, Bean. We will go to our mother. You are my family!"

Bean kneeled and lifted her chin. "Nell, you're a Human. While we share the same mother, you're not my kin. Whether you fight back or not, I *will* kill you."

His eerie, calm voice and composed face—both devoid of emotion—sent a shiver down her back.

"Where is my mother?" she asked quietly.

"You'll never see her, sister."

Bean lifted his sword, preparing to attack her. Then he hissed in a sharp breath, his eyes wide with surprise, and the sword dropped from his grip.

Nell released the short dagger that she had plunged into his heart and he slumped forward. She let out a cry and gathered him in her lap, rocking him gently. A gurgle of bright blood slid down the corner of his mouth as he stared at her.

"You hurt me," he croaked in surprise.

Nell's throat burned. "I am sorry, brother."

Bean let out a final ragged breath, his green eyes dead.

She stared down at him, silent for a moment. She thought of all that had happened, how things could have been different. She had had a brother—*family.*

Now I have nothing.

A hand touched her shoulder.

She shook it off, her eyes never leaving her brother.

"We need to go, Nell," Treyton said gently.

When she stood, she did something that surprised them all, including herself. She lifted Bean's lifeless body in her arms.

"My brother will get a proper burial."

Lachlin watched the Garshu sink into the sea. She had taken no injuries, nor had she handed out any. The enemy was whisked away before any could even reach her. There were still a hesitant few near the shoreline and one commander who remained at the edge of the forest, watching his army slowly taken from him.

She studied him now.

When he caught her gaze, he raised a fiery ball in the air and swung it around on a chain. Then he let the bomb loose.

Lachlin followed it with her eyes.

Just moments before it reached her face, the bomb was diverted away. It dove into the water and sizzling steam enveloped it as it bobbed on the surface.

She sucked in a startled gasp.

An arrow had pierced the smouldering ball.

Lachlin's gaze drifted to the forest. "Where are you?"

It had to have been Garick.

Puzzled, she scanned the forest edge.

Nothing moved.

Except the Garshulan. He scowled at her, but it was obvious he was afraid.

"Attack her!" he ordered.

Some of the Garshu on the shore stepped into the sea, but were immediately sucked underwater. One by one, the Garshulan sent his soldiers to their demise.

After what seemed like an eternity, the Garshulan halted his soldiers. He strolled toward Lachlin, but stopped clear of where the water washed the warm sands.

"Ssseekra! How isss this magic done?"

Lachlin smiled sweetly. "Come closer, you scum, and I will show you."

With horror on their features, Peter and Karistaal

stared at Bean's body on the ground. Peter clenched both fists, while Karistaal stood behind him, one hand on his shoulder, the other muffling her weeping. She swayed with pure grief as the reality of Bean's death slowly sank in.

"Our boy is dead," she sobbed.

Peter nodded, knowing that although his wife had not birthed the boy, she had thought of him like her own. So had he, for that matter. Another child for them to outlive.

He glanced at Nell.

She stood near Bean's head, her hand resting lightly on the sword that she had driven into the ground.

Her brother's sword.

"When this is all over, we will bury him here," Nell said. "We will speak Achocran prayers to Saros, begging the Goddess to forgive his wrongdoings."

She plucked a strand of hair from her head and tied it around the hilt of Bean's sword. She hoped her friends would pray for her own spirit—that she would be forgiven for taking her brother's life, even if it *was* in self defence.

The others held back, waiting for Nell to be satisfied.

Liam's injury proved to be merely a flesh wound. Treyton had wrapped a shirt around his middle to staunch the bleeding, and now Liam was standing on a forested rise overlooking the beach.

"I see them!" he hissed. "And I see Lachlin!"

Stroking the hilt of Bean's sword one last time, Nell strode away from her brother's body, suppressing all the demons that dwelled within her mind—her mother's whereabouts, Bean's wasted life and the murderous Garshu.

She and the others joined Liam. They watched in horror as the Garshu stepped into the water and made their way toward Lachlin, who waited, unmoving, waist-deep in the sea.

Without warning, the once formidable Garshu were sucked under by individual waves and swept away with the tide.

Nell gasped. "What is happening?"

Before anyone could answer, a flaming fireball whistled toward Lachlin. It was immediately struck down by an arrow.

Garick lunged forward. "Where did that come from?"

All eyes gaped at him.

"Wasn't that your arrow?" Liam demanded.

Garick shook his head.

Nell flicked Treyton an uneasy look. "We are not alone."

They followed her through the trees and edged closer to the beach. They did not stop until they spotted a cart camouflaged by bushes. A cloaked figure was hiding in the dense underbrush, watching the beach. His back was to them.

"I know him," Treyton muttered. "I saved that ruddy Elf. I can't believe he followed us all the way out here."

Nell nodded. "Aye, I know him too. He was the one who warned me of the Garshu near our camp at Follok." She pursed her lips and rubbed her forehead. "What did he say his name was?"

Her question was carried on the wind.

The Elf whirled around, his face concealed by the hood. When he saw them, the bow in his hand dropped to the ground and a stifled gasp was heard. Then he took a step forward and tossed back his hood.

It took Nell a moment to realize that the Elf was staring at one person in their group—Garick. She opened her mouth to say something, but the bewildered expression on her guardian's face made her snap it shut.

"Hello, brother," the scrawny Elf said.

Stunned, Garick dropped to his knees, unable to utter a word as he gulped for air. He crawled toward his brother, clung to him in disbelief and shook fiercely as sorrow engulfed him.

"Dintik, I am so sorry!"

Dintik placed a shaky hand on Garick's head. "Weep no more, brother. I have found you."

Garick lifted his head. "Forgive me. Please forgive

me."

"I do," Dintik whispered.

The older Elf sobbed harder.

"Stand, brother," Dintik said, wiping a tear from his eye.

Reluctantly, Garick clambered to his feet.

"I thought you were dead," Dintik said.

Garick laughed. "Aye, and I *you.*"

They embraced.

When they separated, Garick shook his brother's shoulder lovingly. "You have aged well. You look like father."

"Aye, but not as much as you."

Nell's throat burned as she watched the bittersweet reunion, thankful that the rigid shell around her guardian had cracked and revealed the Garick she loved so much.

Behind her, Liam cleared his throat. "Sorry, Garick, my friend. Perhaps we should—just for now—divert our attention back to...er, matters at hand. Something is taking any who touch the water. Well, except for Lachlin, that is." He looked at Dintik. "I assume I have you to thank for diverting that bomb from my sister."

The Elf patted Garick's back. "I had a good teacher."

A deafening roar thundered in the air.

Parting the bushes, Nell watched in horror as the Garshu began charging down the beach toward Lachlin. A lone Garshulan remained near the tree line; weapon in hand, his eyes intently on Lachlin.

Garick huddled close to Nell. When his gaze fell upon the Garshulan, he stiffened and his face grew furious.

"What is wrong?" she asked.

"That is the same Garshulan from the raid on Paraan. The one who slit that little Elf girl's throat."

Treyton leaned forward. "Let's return the favour."

"He seems nervous," Nell observed. "Do you think he knows we are here?"

Garick shook his head. "It matters not. He is mine!"

When he slipped through the bushes, Nell wanted to call him back, but she knew that he would not be stopped. She watched with bated breath as he crept behind the Garshulan. He lunged forward, throwing himself at the leader's back.

The Garshulan let out a startled yelp.

The small dagger that Garick drew across his throat quickly silenced it. In one single swipe, the Garshulan's head was nearly separated from his body.

Lachlin saw the Garshulan drop lifelessly from Garick's arms. She let out a sigh of relief. Her friends had made it.

A few paces away, the last remaining Garshulan was swallowed by the hungry sea and she waded back to shore. As she stepped onto the sand, a wispy wave followed her, grasping, reaching for her skin.

Not yet!

"Garick!" she yelled. "Where is everyone?"

In answer, everyone emerged from the forest and hurried toward the beach.

Lachlin smiled. "You're all safe."

"Thanks to you," Nell said, hugging her. "Whatever you did to lure the Garshu, it worked. They are all dead. *And* the Garshulas." She placed a hand on Lachlin's arm. "We did it."

The tide rose swiftly, washing over their ankles.

"No!" Lachlin wailed, falling to her knees.

Nell caught her. "Are you injured?"

"The water…"

Nell hurriedly pulled her from the sea. She dragged her up the beach and collapsed in the sand, with Lachlin slumped across her lap.

Lachlin's breathing was laboured. Her skin began to quiver and the red scar around her neck burst open, spilling not blood but salty water all over chest.

Liam crouched at her side. "Oh, Lachlin."

He glared at Nell. "What happened?"

"I-I do not know. She was just—"

Nell's knees became damp. When she looked down, she saw a large pool of water in the sand. She frowned.

Then her eyes drifted toward Lachlin.

Oh, Saros. No!

Lachlin was dissolving, liquefying before their very eyes.

"What did you do to her, Nell?" Liam demanded.

"No," Lachlin whispered. "It was the Merfolk. I gave them a life bind, remember?"

"Why would you do that?" he cried.

"To save you. When you almost drowned years ago."

Liam held her hand. "We could have defeated the Garshu some other way."

"There *was* no other way, Liam. I had to go into the water. It was the only way to get the Garshu out of the caves." She writhed in agony. "They're taking me, brother. I had to do it…for all of you."

Lachlin attempted a smile. "We did it though. We defeated them. It's only a matter of time before all the Garshu armies are—" she moaned, "wiped out."

"But why, Lachlin?" Liam cried. "You could've stayed away from the sea forever."

Lachlin gazed at Nell. "I did it because she has to live. Because Treyton loves her."

She gasped and her legs dissolved into the sand.

"And because I love you." Her eyes found Treyton's. "Both of you."

It was over in an instant. All that was left of Lachlin was a puddle of crystal water that glittered in the moonlight. Then, drawn by the power of the Merfolk, the puddle trickled down the beach and merged with the sea.

"No!" Liam roared. "Come back!"

He ran to the edge of the beach, but Treyton restrained him before the sea could capture yet another soul.

No one else said a word.

Karistaal and Peter clutched each other, shaken by what they had witnessed. Garick and Dintik hovered over Nell, neither knowing quite what to do, or say.

Nell stood, silently acknowledging Lachlin's gift.

As a child, Lachlin had sacrificed herself for her brother. Now she had done so for all of them, for Nell and for Treyton.

Nell blinked back burning tears. "Why does so much sacrifice—so much death—have to occur in order for life and love to triumph?"

A single wave lapped the shore, as if in answer.

Epilogue

The new dawn brought a faint light into the Garshula's lair. A rumble of thunder shook the walls of the cave and the dead mass shifted. From beneath the decaying carcass of the Garshula, one white egg rolled free.

It waited, fermenting.

Soon it would be time to hatch.

Nell was dreaming again, the same horrifying dream that continued to haunt her.

Now she knew to whom the metal boots belonged.

She also knew it meant the war was not over.

It was just beginning.

THE LAST FOREVER
BOOK TWO

SURVIVAL

Be sure to watch for the
second novel by
Kelly Komm—
the intense conclusion of
THE LAST FOREVER

WWW.KELLYKOMM.COM